"You know more than you're telling."

Suddenly Riley was backing her against the wall. The heat from his body scorched Devra's skin right through the stiff cotton fabric of her dress. His dark eyes filled her vision and clouded her mind.

"What are you hiding?" he said softly, the rich timbre of his voice stroking sensitive nerve endings.

"Nothing."

"Then why are you hiding?" he whispered, and speared his fingers through her hair, lifting, and letting it tumble across her shoulders.

Devra couldn't get enough air. Her skin burned and a yearning deep in the pit of her stomach made her want to scream.

"Leave me alone," she pleaded, knowing full well she wanted him to pull her up against him and smother her lips with a kiss so passionate it could rip the fabric of her being.

I can't afford to let anyone get too close. Especially this man....

Dear Harlequin Intrigue Reader,

Spring is in the air and we have a month of fabulous books for you to curl up with as the March winds howl outside:

- Familiar is back on the prowl, in Caroline Burnes's *Familiar Texas*. And *Rocky Mountain Maneuvers* marks the conclusion of Cassie Miles's COLORADO CRIME CONSULTANTS trilogy.

- Jessica Andersen brings us an exciting medical thriller, *Covert M.D.*

- Don't miss the next ECLIPSE title, Lisa Childs's *The Substitute Sister.*

- Definitely check out our April lineup. Debra Webb is starting THE ENFORCERS, an exciting new miniseries you won't want to miss. Also look for a special 3-in-1 story from Rebecca York, Ann Voss Peterson and Patricia Rosemoor called *Desert Sons.*

Each month, Harlequin Intrigue brings you a variety of heart-stopping romantic suspense and chilling mystery. Don't miss a single book!

Sincerely,

Denise O'Sullivan
Senior Editor
Harlequin Intrigue

SHIVER

CYNTHIA COOKE

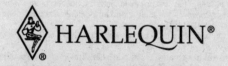

HARLEQUIN®

TORONTO • NEW YORK • LONDON
AMSTERDAM • PARIS • SYDNEY • HAMBURG
STOCKHOLM • ATHENS • TOKYO • MILAN • MADRID
PRAGUE • WARSAW • BUDAPEST • AUCKLAND

To my editor, Kim Nadelson, for seeing the gem buried
within the rock. To my critique partners, you're the best!
And, as always, to my family—I love you!!

ISBN 0-373-22836-8

SHIVER

Copyright © 2005 by Cynthia D. Cooke

This edition published by arrangement with Harlequin Books S.A.

® and TM are trademarks of the publisher. Trademarks indicated with
® are registered in the United States Patent and Trademark Office, the
Canadian Trade Marks Office and in other countries.

www.eHarlequin.com

Printed in U.S.A.

ABOUT THE AUTHOR

Ten years ago, Cynthia Cooke lived a quiet, idyllic life caring for her beautiful eighteen-month-old daughter. Then peace gave way to chaos with the birth of her boy/girl twins. Hip-deep in diapers and baby food and living in a world of sleep deprivation, she kept her sanity by reading romance novels and dreaming of someday writing one. She counts her blessings every day as she fulfills her dreams with the love and support of good friends, her very own hunky hero and three boisterous children who constantly keep her laughing and her world spinning. Cynthia loves to hear from her readers. Visit her online at www.cynthiacooke.com.

Books by Cynthia Cooke

HARLEQUIN INTRIGUE
836—SHIVER

LOVE INSPIRED
238—LUCK AND A PRAYER
275—PETER'S RETURN

CAST OF CHARACTERS

Riley MacIntyre—A detective determined to discover who murdered his sister-in-law, even if that means getting really close to his number one suspect, Devra Morgan. As the case deepens and the mystery evolves, he will have to decide if she belongs in prison or in his arms.

Devra Morgan—She watched her childhood friend, Tommy Marshall, die in a horrible act of violence. Wherever she goes, death follows her as women who look like her fall prey to a killer. And she sees it all—in her dreams.

Michelle MacIntyre—A cop working undercover to flush out the night stalker runs into a new monster and loses her life.

Tommy Marshall—Devra's first crush, first kiss—then he was dead.

Mac MacIntyre—Is he a grieving husband or a man bent on an elaborate plot to kill his wife?

Mr. MacIntyre—The head of the MacIntyre clan—whose strings does he pull?

Chief Marshall—A small-town police chief whose only child was murdered fifteen years earlier by Devra—or so he believes. He will stop at nothing to bring her to justice.

William and Lydia Miller—Best-kept secrets can be fatal. What exactly do they know? And why are they so anxious for Devra to leave her childhood home?

Chapter One

Thunder boomed overhead and electricity crackled through the air, prickling the hair on the nape of Detective Riley MacIntyre's neck. The large drops of rain wetting his shoulders didn't relieve the stickiness of the hot August night as he approached the crime scene. Someone yelled for a cover and umbrellas were quickly opened above the body. Then a tarp was stretched over the area.

Sweat, partly from the heat and partly in expectation of what he'd find, ran down Riley's back, further dampening his shirt as pulsing red and blue lights flashed on and off centuries-old brick in a strange melodic symphony. He stepped over the yellow caution tape encircling the crime scene and made his way toward the group of people congregating in front of the Village Carré Hotel.

Mike Parker, a young officer from the Eighth District, approached him, his footsteps matching beat for beat the music echoing down Bourbon Street. "We have everything under control, Detective MacIntyre." A hint of wariness creased his eyes. "We can handle this. You don't need to be here."

Riley cocked a smile but couldn't quite soften the edge of annoyance in his voice. "The last time I checked, this was my case."

"We haven't established if this is part of the night stalker case. This one is, uh…different." Parker looked down, fidgeting.

Riley frowned. "You obviously need some time off, 'cause you're not making any sense. All homicides are handled downtown. You know that. It doesn't matter if it's related to the night stalker case or not." He patted Parker's shoulder, then strode off, annoyed that his routine crime-scene approach had been thwarted. He liked to walk a scene to get a sense of the perimeter—the sounds, sights, smells—before approaching the victim. Sometimes the brutality of murder deadened his perceptions. Then all was lost, his case compromised.

He tried once again to recapture the scene, absorbing the music, the scent of onions and garlic and simmering jambalaya, a constant yet comforting smell in the French Quarter. As he approached the building, a roach popped out of a broken stone tile in the sidewalk, then scurried into a cracked grate.

In the crevice between the structure's brick wall and the steep cement steps leading into a doorway, a body leaned haphazardly, the face hidden beneath a thick mass of blond curls. Blue-jean-clad long legs stretched out on the sidewalk. His gaze lingered over turquoise spiked heels adorning perfectly shaped feet. His gut twisted; sweat dampened his palms.

He took a step closer, though for the first time in his career something urged him to turn away—some gut instinct that was his strongest, most prized possession as a detective in the New Orleans Police Department. He looked back at Parker, who was still watching him, shifting from one foot to the other.

Something wasn't right.

He took another step. Tony Tortorici, his friend and partner, stood from his examination of the victim. Suddenly, Riley could see her clearly—her deep purple shirt, loops of bright beads hanging from her neck. Pulse racing, he saw how two strands of gold-and-green plastic dice were entwined tightly around her neck, pushing into her delicate skin.

His breathing went shallow as he took in the ugly purple-red bruises beneath the beads and the gold locket lying snug between her breasts. Tony walked toward him, his arms hanging limp at his sides, his eyes filled with sympathy. Riley couldn't move, couldn't swallow, couldn't draw enough of the thick, foul air into his lungs.

He focused on the thick mass of blond hair, hair that he remembered could look like silk billowing in the wind. A sharp twinge shot through him. In her lap, her hands, crossed one over the other, rested against the light blue fabric of her shirt, her pinkies interlaced. The position was strange, but before he could think on it further, his eyes locked on the contrasting colors between the top and the bottom of her shirt.

Pain surged through him, slicing his heart as surely as the killer had sliced her throat, turning the blue fabric dark purple with her blood. Blood that had pumped from a heart he'd known since childhood.

"I'm so sorry, man," Tony said as he reached him.

The compassion on Tony's face hit Riley like a blow to the stomach. Anguish loosened his neck muscles and his head rolled back. He stared into the night sky. Drops of rain pelted his face as agony welled up inside him and broke free in a heart-wrenching roar.

Michelle.

DEVRA MORGAN dreamed of death again—another blue-eyed blonde. She sat up with a start, her heart beating against her chest, her breath coming fast and hard. She brought two shaking fingers to the soft skin of her throat almost expecting to feel a deep gash and the sticky warmth of blood.

Her cat, Felix, meowed in protest as she threw the covers over him and stumbled to the bathroom. Cold sweat chilled her. The distinct scent of the Quarter, with its heavy air and heady taste of the Mississippi, still lingered in her mind. She stood under the hot spray of the shower, scrubbing until her skin ached.

Why now?

Pulling on a plush white robe, she trudged to the kitchen, put the teakettle on to boil and closed her eyes as an onslaught of chills shook her. She couldn't go through this again. Not now. Not after she'd actually convinced herself they were over—the horrible dreams that had destroyed so much of her life.

She picked up Felix and squeezed him against her chest, burying her chin in his soft fur. "Why is this happening now?" She set him down and opened a can of cat food. "I'll have to move again," she muttered. If she didn't, it wouldn't be long before the police came calling and her world came crashing down around her. *Again.*

She sighed, added a spoonful of honey to her tea and strode toward her office. The quicker she got down on paper what she'd seen in her dream, the sooner she could purge it from her mind. Her writing had become an amazing catharsis over the years. Her only means of escape from her nightmarish reality had turned into her salvation and allowed her the freedom and the anonymity she needed to survive. She sat behind the large white desk, turned on her computer and began to type.

"Hey, lady, looking good tonight. Want me to read your fortune?"

The woman glanced at the tarot card readers and threw the cute one a wave. "No, thanks. Tonight I make my own fortune."

Devra's fingers flew over the keyboard as she slipped into her "zone" where each story overcame her. She typed steadily reliving her dream careful to get down every detail, hoping somehow, some way, her dream would help. Not that they ever had before. Town after town, she had to watch women die and yet was never able to stop it from happening or help find their killers. The dreams always came too late.

He took something gold and shiny and slipped it around her neck. A gold heart with a rose etched across the front dangled between her breasts, nestling amidst the rivulets of blood seeping from her throat.

Devra stopped typing and stared at the words on her screen, her heart pounding anew. She closed her eyes and pictured the locket in her mind. *Her locket?* Her stomach muscles clenched with fear. The one she'd lost last week, the one her parents had given her on her thirteenth birthday. The one with *her* name inscribed on the back.

Her vision swam as she stared at the screen. How had this monster gotten her locket? And why had he left it on that poor girl? Was it a message for her? The realization hit her hard. He stole her locket!

He knew who she was.

THE NEXT MORNING, Riley and his partner sat parked outside a well-kept, small yellow house in the Garden District. Through the plastic bag, he read the word etched on the back of the locket. *Devra.* He turned to his closest friend and partner, Tony Tortorici. "I can't believe you found her so fast."

"Hey, with a name like Devra, tracking her was as easy as slicing into one of Mama's homemade pecan pies."

"What do we know about Miss Morgan?" Riley asked, letting his gaze wander over the manicured lawn and abundant flowers. There was nothing unusual or even rundown about the house, and yet a prickle of anxiety ate away at him.

"Not much. She's clean." Tony inspected her file. "Just moves around a lot."

"For her sake, she'd better be clean." Riley tried to squeeze a character type from the place she lived, but it was nondescript, a typical modest home in the lush Garden District a few blocks down from the opulent mansions that saw a steady stream of tourist traffic.

Concern filled Tony's large Italian eyes. "You shouldn't go in there. You shouldn't even be here now. Go home and be with your family. With Mac."

Riley fought the guilt and weariness that threatened to overcome him at the mention of his brother's name. He squeezed his eyes shut, but the image of his sister-in-law propped against the wall, her throat slit from ear to ear, was painfully etched in his mind. "I can't."

Tony's dark eyes intensified. "You can't blame yourself. It wasn't your fault."

"Wasn't it? Michelle was taking this case too personally."

"You couldn't know she'd go undercover and try to flush the night stalker out alone."

"I knew some sicko was slicing up prostitutes in the Quarter. I should have watched her better. I should have been more—" inwardly, he cringed as he said the word "—protective."

"She would have been insulted, and she would have thought you doubted her abilities as a cop. You know that. You also know if you go in there and confront Miss Morgan, you could blow this investigation."

"You're right. But Tony, Michelle was family." A lump the size of a crawdad caught in his throat. "I should have done something. If only—"

"Michelle was a strong-willed cop. She did what she wanted and damn the consequences. You knew that about her, and so did Mac."

Riley scraped a thumb across his unshaven jaw. "I'm going to track this guy down. I won't let him get by with this. And I won't blow this case." His gaze drifted over the roses, blooming in a riot of color lining the walk. "I'll turn on 'Mr. Charm.' I'll be on my best behavior. I just need to see for myself how she responds when I show her the locket."

Tony closed the file and slid it between the seats. "All right," he relented. "Two of us will spook her. I've been up all night tracking down Miss Morgan and I'm in desperate need of some caffeine. You're on your own. I'll be back in fifteen minutes. Don't blow it!"

"Wouldn't dream of it." Riley opened the car door. "I'll find out exactly what she knows about Michelle's death. Whatever it takes."

"That's what I'm afraid of," Tony muttered, and pulled away from the curb.

Although it was only 9:00 a.m., the hot August heat was already intolerable. Riley walked toward the front door, pulling at his shirt collar, lifting the fabric from his skin. He rapped on the door, waited a minute, then rapped again.

He stood on the front stoop listening to the incessant buzz of bees surrounding a gardenia bush, growing hotter and more impatient with each passing second. As he started to knock again, a shape moved behind the front door's frosted glass.

"Finally," he muttered under his breath.

The door opened. His wide "Mr. Charm" smile froze on his face and his heart stopped at the sight of the woman in the white terry robe. A mass of golden curls framed her face, falling in reckless abandon around her shoulders. Blue eyes, tired and disoriented, held a dim sparkle deep within their depths.

Michelle.

"Is there something I can do for you?" she asked, clutching the opening of her robe.

Her sultry voice held no hint of Michelle's Southern accent. Otherwise, she looked enough like Michelle to halt the blood in his veins. "Devra Morgan?" he asked and wasn't at all surprised by the catch in his voice.

"Yes?"

He couldn't help staring. She clutched the robe tighter. "I'm Detective MacIntyre with the NOPD. Is this yours?" He held up the plastic bag containing the golden locket in one hand, and his badge in the other.

Her eyes widened, turning a deep cobalt blue and becoming even more beautiful than he'd previously thought. "Wh-where did you find it?" she asked.

"May I come in?"

"Yes, of course. I'm sorry. Come in." She stood back, allowing him to step into the entryway. He followed her into a darkened living room. The furniture was sparse with no plants, no pictures, not much of anything personal or otherwise.

"Please, have a seat," she offered, and gestured toward a small table in front of the window. As he sat, she reached behind him and pulled the cord that lifted thick wooden blinds. Sunshine filtered through the slats, setting fire to the gold in her hair.

She smelled faintly of vanilla and he caught himself inhaling deeper. He couldn't stop staring at her hair falling in long lazy curls down the middle of her back. He was sorely tempted to touch it, to run his fingers through the delicate strands.

She looked down at him, catching his gaze. Her eyes flickered with a myriad of colors and emotions. There was a longing in her expression—something she wanted or needed—but it quickly disappeared and her expression turned wary. She ran a hand through her hair. "Would you excuse me for a minute, please?"

He nodded and watched the soft sway of her hips as she turned the corner. While at first glance her resemblance to Michelle was overwhelming, she was different in many ways—her walk, her height, the flawless texture of her skin and her lips. Michelle's lips had been thin and expressive, but this woman's were wide and luscious. Lips made for devouring.

He stood, annoyed at his thoughts, and pushed them from his mind. Obviously, he was tired and not thinking too clearly. He began a preliminary search of the room, just to get a handle on the woman and what she was about. Opening an old cabinet in the corner, he found a television, TV program guide and a remote control. No bills, coupons, cassette tapes, film canisters—nothing like the clutter in his house.

The mantel above the fireplace held only an old clock, the kind in a glass dome that chimed on the hour. He passed through a doorway into the kitchen and found the same bold emptiness. Had she just moved in? He pulled open a few drawers, but found only bare-essential kitchen items.

"Looking for something?" she asked, her voice low and sultry with an edge of what? Irritation? Fear?

He shut the drawer and turned ready to give her his best "hand-caught-in-the-cookie-jar" excuse, but his words died on his lips. Her glorious mane of hair had been twisted severely back across her head, and large glasses covered her eyes and half her face.

The white robe was gone, too, replaced by a dull, gray sleeveless smock. She'd transformed herself into someone no one would ever notice. As he stared at her, he was finding it hard to believe she was the same sexy woman who'd just left the room. What was with the getup? Why was a beautiful woman hiding beneath such an ugly facade?

"I'm sorry, Miss Morgan. I'm afraid I've let my curiosity overcome my good manners," he drawled, letting his accent roll heavily off his tongue.

She raised a skeptical brow.

"I know it must be hard to believe someone you just caught snooping in your drawers has good manners, but my mama would've been remiss if she didn't pound those Southern manners into me every day of my rebellious life." He gave her that famous MacIntyre grin, known to melt butter in frying pans and sizzle any lady's heart. Well, except maybe this one. She wasn't biting any more than a gator in December.

"What can I do for you, Mr…?"

"Detective MacIntyre," he repeated.

She nodded, her eyes turning frostier by the moment.

"How long have you lived here?" he asked.

"What does that have to do with my locket?"

"First things first, all right?"

"I don't understand," she hedged.

"Please answer the question."

"Three years."

He looked around, disbelieving. "In this house?"

"Yes."

"Don't believe in too many possessions, do you, Miss Morgan?"

"May I have my locket?"

"I'm afraid not." He propped himself against the wall and crossed his arms against his chest.

"And why's that?"

Was that a quiver in her voice? "Evidence."

Her gaze shifted down and her small white fingers fluttered like a butterfly as she played with the top button on her dress. "When, then, may I have it?"

"Don't you want to know why it's being held?"

A shadow passed in front of her eyes. She mouthed something, then dropped her hands to the counter between them.

He stepped closer to her, determined to discover what had her so fidgety. "I'm sorry. I didn't catch that."

"No. I don't," she blurted.

"Now I find that mighty strange." He took another step toward her, placed both hands on either side of hers and leaned in close. Close enough to see the creamy white skin of her throat flutter as she swallowed. "Why wouldn't you want to know what happened to an obviously cherished possession?"

She took a step back, refusing to meet his eyes.

"Most people would," he continued. "Why not you?"

She didn't respond. Just stared at the floor between her toes and wrung those small white fingers. Fingers that could have slit Michelle's throat? He was finding that difficult to believe, but she was afraid of something.

"Is there some point to all this, Detective MacIntyre?"

Her lower lip quivered, and he felt an urge to reach out his thumb and still it. "What do you do, Miss Morgan?"

"Excuse me?"

"For work?"

"I write."

"A writer, huh? What do you write?"

"Would you like some coffee? Iced tea?" she asked.

"Tea would be great." He leaned against the kitchen counter, kicking one boot over the other, and watched as she passed, sorely tempted to blow on the fine hairs that had slipped their bondage to feather against the back of her neck. He forced back the thought and considered how hard he should push for the answers to the questions she was so obviously evading.

She opened the fridge, removed a large pitcher of tea and filled two glasses. She placed a glass in front of him, along with a bowl of sugarcoated pecans.

"Thank you, ma'am. That's mighty hospitable of you."

Without looking at him, she picked up a pecan and bit into it. A dab of sugar creased the corner of her sweet little mouth. The tip of her tongue peeked out and licked the sugar away. The movement warmed the chill in his blood. He ignored it and gulped down his tea. Her large luminous eyes watched him, looking vulnerable one moment and calculating the next. This was a woman with a secret. One way or another, he was going to discover what that secret was.

DEVRA TOOK a deep breath to steady herself. She turned her back on the rude detective to return the tea to the fridge. She needed to stay calm, to give nothing away. Her hair tickled the back of her neck, sending an uncomfortable heat racing through her. He was staring at her again, with a look so intense she was sure he could see right through her.

She closed her eyes. Breathe—in and out, in and out. She tried to ignore the intense gleam in his eyes and the hard lines sculpturing his jaw. They made her anxious. They made him look as if he could become unhinged at any moment.

"So, what type of stuff do you write?" he asked, pinning her with another of his dark, primitive stares.

"All types," she muttered, and dropped her gaze to wide shoulders tapering down to a narrow waist where tight jeans molded thick thighs. With dark blond hair and eyes as brown and rich as a cup of espresso at Emeril's, the combined effect definitely made the man a risk. She'd have to be extra careful around this one. He could do too much to her senses without even trying.

"Published?"

"Enough to make a living." She watched under lowered lashes as he popped a few more pralines and drank down his tea in large gulps. He exuded an overabundance of confidence and moved with the grace of a panther. A dangerous mix, and she had a good idea he could be equally ferocious.

A trickle of moisture ran between her shoulder blades. She glanced at the clock. "Look, I've got to go soon. Are we about done?"

His gaze, cool and assessing, studied her. "A young woman—twenty-five, blond, beautiful, married and happy—her whole life in front of her, was found dead in the Quarter with this around her neck." He held up the plastic baggie containing Devra's locket.

But she couldn't look at the necklace; she was too focused on the man's eyes, the deep brown of them melting in pain. He'd known this woman well. "I'm sorry," she offered, though she understood it wasn't enough.

It never was.

His eyes narrowed and his pretense of charm and suaveness disappeared, replaced by something uglier, something desperate and frustrated. "I want to know how this necklace wound up around her neck." He slammed his glass onto the counter. She jumped, refusing to meet his eyes. There was nothing she could offer that would help him or that woman.

"When was the last time you saw your necklace?" He was close—too close—stealing her energy, her breath, her feeble hold on her senses.

She stared at the locket through the plastic, focusing on the small rose etched on its face, on anything but him. "Last Saturday, at the Children's Hospital."

"You sure?"

"Yes. I mean…I think I am."

"Can you think of any reason why your necklace would have been found on a murder victim?"

Because I'm next? "No," she whispered. She looked up at him, her gaze colliding with his. Big mistake. His doubt, his anger, riding so close to the surface, frightened her. "I don't know. Maybe she found it," she offered in a voice barely above a whisper.

"No one has ever seen her with it before. Plus, it has a picture in it of a couple I've never seen. I know her. She wouldn't wear a locket with someone else's picture in it."

Devra nodded slowly. Of course she wouldn't.

"Who are they? The couple in the picture."

She hesitated, her tongue seeming to thicken and fill her mouth.

He stepped closer. She could smell him now…rich, spicy, male.

"Who are they?" he repeated.

"My parents."

"Where do they live?"

"Washington State."

He pulled a notepad out of his back pocket. "Their names?"

She hesitated.

He looked at her, waiting, coldly calculating.

She said the names she hadn't uttered in fifteen years. "William and Lydia." *William and Lydia Miller.* But she wouldn't tell him that much, not if she could help it. He closed the notepad and shoved it back into his pocket. She let out the breath she'd been holding and waited for him to back away.

He didn't.

"Is that all?" she stammered.

His piercing gaze looked right through her. "Is there anything else you'd like to tell me?"

"Like what?"

"Do you have a record?"

An ice pick of fear pierced her heart and sent a cold shiver pulsing through her. She knew what was coming, knew what he'd ask next. He stepped closer stealing her air. "Have you ever been arrested?"

Chapter Two

Every natural-born cop instinct Riley had sang in tune. "Why are you rubbing your wrists?"

She didn't answer and refused to look at him.

A telltale sign? His adrenaline kicked into high gear. "You won't mind coming downtown to answer a few more questions, perhaps take a set of fingerprints?"

Her eyes shot to his. "What on earth for? I didn't have anything to do with this woman's murder. I didn't even know her."

"How do you know you didn't know her? I haven't shown you her picture yet."

"Because I don't know very many people here," she said defensively and started to pace the room. "And I certainly don't know any female police officers." She stopped and looked at him with cold fear widening her eyes.

Gotcha, sweetheart. "I don't believe I mentioned the young woman was a cop."

She just stood there, staring at him.

"Right about now an explanation would be good," he prompted. "How did you know she was a cop?"

A loud knock at the front door reverberated through the house. Devra jumped. Riley swore under his breath. "That would be my partner."

"Oh," she murmured, looking scared and relieved at the same time. He was aware of her soft step as she followed him through the living room and toward the front door.

How had this woman known Michelle was a cop? She'd been working undercover. Any bystander would have thought she was a prostitute. This woman knew a lot more than she was letting on. All he needed was a little more time alone with her and he'd have her singing.

He stood back and allowed her to open the door. Tony strode in, looking flushed and wiping the sweat off his brow. "It's hotter than Hades out there. Are you about done here? The captain just called and said he wants to see you pronto."

Riley turned. "Devra Morgan, Detective Tortorici. Grab your purse, looks like we're going downtown."

Tony raised a questioning brow.

She sputtered a protest, outrage crossing her face. "I can't go. I'm due at the Children's Hospital for story time. I have to be there."

"I'm sure they can find someone else to read *Green Eggs and Ham* this morning."

Unyielding, she stood with her hands braced on her hips. "No. There isn't anyone else. The nurses are too busy. The children look forward to my being there. It's important to them and to me."

Her sudden display of backbone interested him. Was

it disappointing the kids that had her all charged up, or the fear of going to the station?

Tony stepped forward. "Why don't I accompany Miss Morgan to the hospital, then bring her by the station when she's done?" He offered one of his smooth Italian smiles. "That way, Riley, you can go see the captain and she can still read to the kiddies." He gestured wide with his hands.

Always the diplomat, Riley thought, but this time it wasn't going to fly. "I'll take her to the hospital," he insisted. "We'll come in to the station right after."

Tony's mouth twisted with disapproval.

"I'll get my purse," Devra said.

Riley watched her hurry down the hall. Once she rounded the corner, he lowered his voice. "Look, Tony. You and I both know what the captain is going to say the moment I walk through the door."

"Yeah, what I already told you this morning. You shouldn't be working this case. You're too involved to be objective."

"Exactly. That's why I'm going to accompany Miss Morgan to the hospital. She knows something and she's this close to breaking." He pushed his thumb and forefinger close together. "I won't let her out of my sight. After she's done, I'll bring her in to give her statement."

"And what am I supposed to tell the captain?"

"You'll think of something. I can't let this slippery little fish slither off the line. Not after I so expertly baited the hook. She knows something, Tony, and I mean to get it out of her."

As RILEY parked the car, Miss Morgan leapt out and all but ran to the front of the building. He followed her into the hospital, easily keeping pace. She could run, but she couldn't hide the truth from him for very long. Discovering secrets and solving mysteries were his forte and he wasn't about to let this case be any different. He entered the sliding glass doors and followed her into the elevator.

She pressed the button for the fifth floor, then kept her gaze glued to the flashing lights as they rose. "How long have you been coming here?" he asked, trying to get her to open up. The more she talked, the more that deep sultry voice of hers gave away.

"Three years," she answered without taking her eyes off the illuminated panel.

"Impressive."

She didn't respond.

"Which floor is the cafeteria on?"

She turned, irritation pursing her lips.

"You know. Coffee?"

"I don't know. I've never been."

"Don't eat or drink?"

She turned back to the doors, ignoring him. He smiled at the back of her head. He was getting to her, making her mad. That's when she'd give away the game. He'd give her a little line, let her think she was slipping away, then jerk back and reel her in.

The doors opened.

Placing a hand on her rigid elbow, he walked her to the door of the Child Life Center where a group of kids—some in pajamas, some in wheelchairs, some sitting on the floor—was expectantly awaiting her arrival. He tightened his grip before she could enter the ward. "Can I trust you alone for a minute? I need a cup of joe."

Her gaze shifted slightly, and he knew she was considering bolting. But she nodded, her eyes locked on his, a beseeching vulnerability shining in their dark blue depths. The look unsettled him. She'd looked that way earlier, like a lost and scared kitten stuck high in a tree. And, for a minute, he wanted to rescue her, to cuddle her.

To protect her.

But he wasn't in the protection business. No matter how tempting the idea sounded, no matter how tempting she was playing Little Miss Scared and Innocent, he would bet his lunch money she was anything but.

She pulled free from his grasp and entered the room, smiling briefly at one of the nurses. It was a nice smile that brightened her whole face. He watched as she transformed once again into a different person—warm and friendly, with sincere hugs and bright smiles. No little lost kitty here.

He was about to leave when a nurse with bouncy brown curls and a white cotton shirt stretched tight across her breasts walked into the hall, shutting the door behind her. "Are you waiting for Devra?" she asked.

He nodded, and smiled as he read the name tag pinned to her blouse. "I sure am, Betty."

She smiled back, deepening her dimples to craters. "She's wonderful with the kids. They really look forward to her visits."

He leaned against the wall. "How long has she been coming?"

"Every Saturday for years now. She's never missed a day." She glanced over her shoulder at Devra through the glass. "The kids are very important to her, and vice versa. We're lucky to have her."

"She's a very special person," he drawled. "But then I think anyone who devotes their life to helping people is special," he added, cranking his Irish charm up a notch.

"Aren't you sweet to say so," she cooed and flapped her hand at his shoulder.

"And Devra," he prompted. "She's just so busy with…"

"Oh, yes. Her writing, I know what you mean. And she must be a very good writer, too."

"Really? Have you read…"

Betty's mouth puckered into a pretty pout. "No, she promised to bring something in, but it must have slipped her mind. And I didn't find anything under her name, so I assume she uses a pseudonym. I keep forgetting to ask her what it is, though." She brightened. "Do you know what it is?"

"No." He paused. "I just thought since you said how good she is…"

"Oh, well she must be because she entrances the kids so. They retell her stories to one another at night before they go to sleep, changing the endings and the characters, acting them out, just as Devra has encouraged them to do. And sometimes, for these kids, that kind of distraction is just what they need."

"She sounds like a saint," he said dryly.

The nurse laughed. "Saint Devra. Has a nice ring to it."

Too bad he was having so much trouble hearing it. "She must have a lot of admirers. Other than the kids," he prompted.

"Well, they certainly do love her. It's funny you mention it, though. In all the time she's been coming, I've never seen her with anyone. And here she's had *two* gentlemen stop by in the past week."

"Two?"

"Oh, yeah. Though, maybe I shouldn't have said anything." A worried look crossed her face as she once again glanced over her shoulder at Devra through the glass.

"It's okay," he assured her. "Miss Morgan and I are just friends." He smiled and dug his hands deep into his pockets, giving her one of those I'm-available-if-you-are looks.

The nurse tilted her head coquettishly. "Well, then, I suppose it's all right if I let the cat out of the bag."

He gave her a wink of encouragement.

"Just last Saturday, a man stood right where you are, watching Devra work with the kids. He didn't say much, just stood there and watched her with this weird expression on his face. He disappeared right before she was done. When I mentioned him to her, she seemed a little surprised and a touch agitated. She was afraid of him, wasn't she? Is that why you're here with her? For her protection?"

Heaven help her if she really did need protection. Look how well he protected Michelle…not to mention his mother. He shook off the thought. More than likely, Devra was agitated because she didn't want anyone linking her with her mystery man. Perhaps an estranged boyfriend? Or an accomplice.

"Can you describe this guy for me?"

"Well…he was ordinary-looking—dark hair, slim, average height. In fact, the only thing memorable about him was his eyes."

"His eyes?"

"Yeah, they were real dark and deep-set—a little intense and spooky-looking. To tell you the truth, he was a little creepy. I could see why Devra would be afraid of him."

"Was she?"

"It wasn't anything she said, just a feeling I had."

Could Miss Morgan have known what the killer was planning? Perhaps he wasn't pushing hard enough. Perhaps it was time to tighten the line. Riley took a picture of Michelle out of his wallet. "Have you seen this woman before?"

The nurse took the picture and studied it for a long moment, then handed it back to him. "Sorry," she said. "She looks a lot like Devra, though."

DEVRA WAS TRYING to concentrate on the children, but found herself hopelessly distracted. *He* was out there flirting with Betty. And Betty was enjoying it, laughing, her perfect curls bouncing, her long red-tipped nails flicking the air as she spoke. And it was bugging Devra to no end, though she couldn't fathom why. She finished another page. She held the book up for the

kids to see the pictures, then caught the detective looking at her. Quickly, she turned the page, and her attention, back to the book.

If she thought about it, she'd have to admit that he
was handsome in a rugged, arrogant kind of way. She
wondered what it would be like to have him look at her
the way he was looking at Betty. But, after a second, she
stopped herself. Thinking about that particular man in
any capacity was dangerous. The sooner she put him out
of her sight and her mind, the better.

She read another page. Someday, she would write
books just for kids and leave the dark, ugly world of her
nightmares far behind her. But, for today, she needed
to say goodbye to the people she would miss the most
when she left New Orleans—the children. Then she
would hurry home, finish packing and disappear. *Again.*

She closed the book, gave the children extra-tight
hugs as she said goodbye, then watched them pile out
of the room. Everyone except Joey. "Did you get your
necklace, Miss Devra?"

Confused, Devra looked down into Joey's eager
gaze. "What necklace is that, sweetie?"

"Your heart necklace."

Her breath caught. *Her locket.* She glanced through
the window into the corridor outside the room, but the
detective was gone. He and Betty must have left to get
that cup of coffee.

"I found it under the chair last week," Joey continued. "I was going to give it to Nurse Jenkins to hold for
you, but your friend said he'd give it to you."

"My friend?"

"Yeah, the man that was here last week."

Devra's heart stilled at his words. She'd forgotten about the man Betty had mentioned. She had convinced herself the nurse had been mistaken. That he'd been waiting for someone else. What if she'd been wrong? What if he had been watching her?

"Did you get it back?" A tinge of anxiousness colored Joey's voice.

Devra bent down so they were eye to eye and offered him a big smile. "I will very soon. Thank you for telling me."

His smile went wide with pride.

"Can you tell me what this man looked like?"

"He was big."

She gave him an encouraging nod. "Uh-huh."

"And dark."

"His skin?"

"No, his hair. And his eyes. He had the darkest eyes I've ever seen. They looked…" He glanced down at his feet, then looked back up at her with uncertainty playing across his gaze. "They looked dead."

Devra recalled seeing eyes like that once. The image flashed through her mind, her stomach turned. She forced a smile through gritted teeth. "Thank you, Joey."

"Joey, it's time for your therapy," a nurse called from the doorway.

Devra waved as he ran through the door to join the nurse. Her knees were beginning to ache and she realized she was still crouched down, her legs locked with an irrational fear. Joey had given her locket to a man with dark eyes. *Dead eyes.*

The eyes of the devil.

She shook off the thought and the fear. Tommy's death had been a lifetime ago and far, far away. It couldn't be the same man.

His killer had never been found.

The thought whispered across her mind. She shivered. The world was full of killers, a fact she knew only too well. Why had this one taken her locket? Had he killed that poor woman and then left the locket for the police to find? But why lead the police to her? Did he know about her dreams? Did he know her secret?

Evil lives within you, child. We need to flush it out.

Tears of frustration filled her eyes. The police would blame her for this woman's death, just like before. Just like Tommy. She had to get away from this town. But first, she had to get away from Detective MacIntyre.

"Miss Morgan?"

His voice pulled her from her thoughts. On trembling knees she stood, smoothing down the front of her dress. Then she looked up into the detective's face. He thought she was a killer, too. That's why he wouldn't leave her alone. He believed she was capable of the unthinkable. Just like everyone else, just like her family.

"Are you all right? Everyone's gone." Concern played around the edges of his voice, but it didn't reach his eyes. He wasn't fooling her. He didn't care. No one did.

She stiffened. "Of course. I'm fine." She walked past him without a second glance. The quicker she got away from him, the better. She kept her head down as she entered the elevator, planning in her mind which boxes she

would pack first, which rooms. By nightfall, she and
Felix would be on the road to a new life. A new beginning. Again.

"Will we be at the station long?" she asked casually.

He looked at her, quiet speculation shining in his
eyes. "Not long."

"Good."

Within twenty minutes, Detective MacIntyre pulled
the blue Expedition into the underground parking structure at the downtown headquarters of the New Orleans
Police Department. But instead of taking her through
the garage entrance, he walked her around to the front
of the building through the main double doors and into
the air-conditioned lobby. The long way.

Devra fidgeted with impatience.

"Hello, Nicci," the detective said and smiled a greet-
ing at the young black woman sitting behind a tall
wooden counter.

"Hey, Riley. I'm sorry to hear about Michelle."

"Thanks," he murmured.

"Please sign in," she said and, without looking at her,
slid a clipboard across the counter.

Devra glanced questioningly at the detective, but he
was too busy flirting with Nicci to notice. She scribbled
her name on the sign-in sheet and slid the clipboard
back across the counter. After another long minute of
flashing teeth and big smiles, MacIntyre finally walked
toward the elevator and pushed the Up button. It was
amazing how women acted around him. Yeah, he was
good-looking, but he was also the most infuriatingly arrogant man she'd ever met.

So what if he resembled Goliath with his bulging biceps and perfect pecs. The man was too cocky for words. He was exactly the kind of man any woman would love to see trip over his own shoelaces. As they entered the elevator, exasperation ballooned inside her. "Is this really necessary? I have things I need to get done today."

"Yes. I believe it is," he said without looking at her. He just stood there with his hands clasped behind his back, staring at the elevator doors.

"I already told you, I didn't kill anyone."

"Yes, you did."

She gritted her teeth and bit back an expletive. She might as well be talking to a huge granite wall. Frustration burned inside her. "In fact, I know that I did lose my necklace at the hospital last Saturday."

"Oh?" His eyebrow lifted a fraction of an inch.

"Yes. Joey, a little boy at story time, told me he found it last week."

"Really," he drawled.

Never had the southern Louisiana accent bothered her more than it did when this man opened his mouth. "Really," she responded and stiffened her legs to keep from stomping her foot.

He turned and pierced her with a look so cold shivers cascaded down her arms. She stepped back, her heartbeat accelerating. It was amazing the effect he had on her. Too bad it wasn't the same effect he seemed to have on all the other women in town.

His eyebrows arched in cold speculation. "You expect me to believe this little boy, Joey, left the hospital in the middle of the night and walked down to the Quarter where he killed an NOPD officer, then hurried back to the hospital. But not before leaving your locket clasped around her neck?"

"Don't be absurd."

"Exactly. I couldn't have said it better myself." He turned as the doors slid open and stepped into the hall.

Could he be any more obtuse? She took a deep breath and followed his long steady gait along the blue-carpeted corridor lined with cubicles on either side. At this point, she didn't care who heard her, she just wanted him to stop and listen. She lunged forward, grabbed his bulging bicep and pulled.

It was like trying to move the Rock of Gibraltar.

"Excuse me," she said through gritted teeth. This time, he stopped, and more than one head popped out from around a partition to see what the ruckus was about. "Joey told me there was a man at the hospital who said he was my friend. Joey believed him when he said he would return the locket to me. So, he gave the locket to the man." She said the words as clearly and as succinctly as she could. Now all she could do was hope there was more to him than bulging biceps and a killer smile. Now all she could do was hope he'd focus on "the man" and leave her alone.

He stepped closer, looking down at her with that piercing gaze that made the oxygen suddenly evaporate from the space she was standing in. "Why didn't you tell me this earlier while we were still at the hospital?"

"I don't know. I guess your charm overwhelmed me and I forgot."

He took another step toward her and, for a second, she thought he was going to throttle her.

"All right, I'll send an officer down to talk to Joey. Maybe he'll remember what the guy looked like."

"Dark eyes," she responded and took a small step back so she wouldn't have to crane her neck. At least, that's the reason she told herself.

"What?"

"Joey said he had really dark eyes."

"Hmm. I'll be sure to write that down."

"Yeah, you wouldn't want to forget."

His jaw stiffened, and she held her breath while waiting for his response, but he didn't answer. He just turned and led her down the hall once more. As they reached a row of desks next to the windows, he pointed to Detective Tortorici. "Would you mind going with Tony down to fingerprinting? I'll type up your statement. You can read it over, sign it, and then I'll take you home."

"Fingerprinting?" she asked, her voice coming out in a squeak.

His eyes narrowed. "Yeah. You have a problem with that?"

She straightened her back and took a deep breath to make sure the squeak was gone. "As a matter of fact, I do. Are you booking me?"

"Did I say I was?"

"Then I don't agree to be fingerprinted."

He blew out an exasperated breath. "Why not? You got something to hide?"

She threw up her hands. "I believe you're trying to

stomp all over my civil liberties, Detective MacIntyre, and I don't like it."

"Really? I thought you were more than willing to help with this case in any way you could."

"I am."

"Except for getting fingerprinted," he said calmly, his gaze cool and slightly disbelieving.

"Exactly." She clenched her teeth, refusing to budge an inch. "So, I really don't see any point in my staying here." She took a step back. "I'm leaving."

"Wait." He latched on to her arm.

She looked down at his hand, then back up into his dark brown eyes. Something lurched inside her—something…uncomfortable. "What?"

He released her and rubbed his face. "I'll drive you."

"I'd rather not."

"It's too hot to walk," he cajoled.

She gave him an icy stare of her own.

"All right," he relented. "If you don't want to be fingerprinted, I can respect that. But can we hang out long enough to get the statement written up? Unless, that is, you don't want to cooperate with the police after all?"

For a second she thought about it, then decided it would be better to cooperate than to have the whole department thinking she had something to hide. "Very well."

"Good, 'cause the process of typing up my notes helps me put my thoughts together and it never fails that I always seem to remember something else to ask. It would help me out a lot if you were here." He smiled at her. That stupid smile he used when he thought he was being charming. But he wasn't. It didn't work on her, not one little bit. She pursed her lips, and tried to rekindle her fading anger.

She gave her statement, then sat quietly as he typed away, his fingers moving awkwardly over the keys and slower than molasses in January. She squeezed her hands together to stop from insisting on typing her statement herself, then looked out the window, examined the clutter on his desk, then looked out the window again, anything to keep from jumping out of her skin with impatience.

Her gaze fell across a picture on his desk—the detective standing between and resting his arms on the shoulders of another man and a woman. Devra's eyes widened as she took in the striking resemblance she shared with this woman—so much more so than with the others. So much more than she remembered from her dream. The sound of typing stopped. She looked up to find the detective staring at her, his eyes hard and unreadable.

"Have you seen that woman before?" he asked.

What could she say? That she'd seen her in a dream with her throat being slashed? They'd lock her up in the nearest loony bin. "She looks like me," Devra stated.

Suspicion teemed in his eyes. And something else... something cold—rage. Fear zipped down her spine.

"And..." he prompted.

"She does look a little familiar," she hedged. "Perhaps I've met her at the hospital. Does she have children?"

"No."

"Oh." She paused, swallowing. "Was she the one who had my locket?"

"In a matter of speaking."

"The woman who was killed?" Nightmarish images flashed behind her eyes—bright beads twisting, pulling taut against white skin, blue eyes bulging with fear. He was getting more and more suspicious by the moment. She could see it in his face, could read it in his eyes. But she didn't know what she could do about it.

Something twitched in his jaw. "Yes, she was."

"I'm sorry," she whispered, unable to meet his gaze.

"So am I."

"Well," she stammered. "Are you almost done?"

"Almost."

Devra turned back to the picture, unable to face the hardness in his face, and noticed the strong resemblance between him and the other man in the picture. "Brother?"

"Yeah. Okay, done." He grabbed the paper out of the printer and thrust it at her.

She scanned it, then signed her name on the bottom.

"Riley, what are you doing?" a man boomed as he walked through the door.

"Just getting a statement, Captain." The detective stood and faced the man, then gestured toward her. "Captain Lewis, this is Devra Morgan. It was her locket we found on Michelle."

Devra stood uncertainly, trying to hide her nervousness.

The captain took only a second to size her up, then

turned back to the detective. "Have Pat finish up her statement. You need some time off. Go home and be with your family."

Devra sat back down and pretended to be reading her statement. He was being taken off the case. She smothered a smile.

"Captain—"

"I don't want any arguments about it," his captain continued. "You're too close to this case to be objective. You could do more harm than good."

"I've been living the night stalker case for thirteen months. I know it inside and out," he insisted.

"At this point, it doesn't matter. This wasn't the night stalker."

"What are you talking about?"

"This one is different, hair and fibers don't match up."

"That's why Michelle was out there. She was trying to flush this guy out. Are you telling me someone else got to her?"

"That's exactly what I'm telling you. Michelle was a good cop. Her death is a terrible loss for all of us. Do yourself a favor, Riley, go home and take care of your family. Take care of yourself."

"There's no way I'm dumping this case," he said softly.

Captain Lewis gestured with the manila file folder clutched in his hand. "You don't have a choice. The FBI is taking over."

"Why?"

The captain glanced at Devra, took the detective by

the arm and led him a few feet away. "The computer matched forensics with three other murders—one each in Portland, San Francisco and Miami. What we have is a killer who goes after blondes—blondes that look a lot like Michelle."

Even though his tone was muted, Devra couldn't help but hear him. Her eyes widened as he listed the cities. Cities she'd lived in. They've found out about the others. It would only be a matter of time before they discovered her connection with those cases, too. But what had he said about forensics?

"Are you saying they were all murdered by the same man?" The detective's voice rose in pitch.

His words didn't make sense. The same man? There was only one killer? The thought and its implications came crashing down around her. Only one? All this time? But she'd thought… It hadn't been the victims she'd been connected to, it'd been him—a killer who murdered women who looked like her.

The room spun. Her stomach heaved. *He'd* known about her all along. *He'd* been following her. Terror seized control of her senses. She stood. She had to leave. Now.

Riley watched his suspect swing her purse over her shoulder and get ready to bolt. She'd heard something. Before she'd gone two steps, he gripped her arm and pulled her back. "What do you know about this case?" he demanded, his barely controlled fury rasping his voice.

"Nothing," she whispered, her eyes widening with the fear of a trapped animal.

"You do!" he insisted. "Tell the truth."

She cringed beneath his fury and fell back into the chair, clutching her purse against her stomach, refusing to meet his gaze—the little scared kitty again.

"Riley!" Captain Lewis warned, outrage crossing his face.

"She's hiding something, Captain." He'd seen it in her face. Something she'd heard had thrown her into a panic. All he needed was another minute to work her and she'd break.

"Get hold of yourself," Captain Lewis demanded.

He wouldn't get hold of himself, he couldn't. His fury was too strong, too pungent; he could taste it with every breath he took. He was so close to the truth. He pulled the folder out of the captain's hands and dumped the contents onto the desk for her to see. Pictures and papers spread haphazardly—pictures of three different women, all with long blond hair cascading in curls around their pale lifeless shoulders.

Pictures of women who looked like Michelle.

Pictures of women who looked like her.

His captain stepped forward. "Riley, we know how much Michelle's death has affected you, but this behavior is unacceptable," he warned. "I shouldn't have to tell you that you're skating on thin ice here, real thin."

"The last murder took place in Miami, three years ago," Riley said, his voice sounding cold and hard. "Where did you live before you came here, Miss Morgan?"

She didn't answer, just stared at him with her round baby-blue eyes trapped in fear.

She should be scared, he thought. Real scared.

By now, everyone in the department was standing, listening, staring with curiosity alive on their faces. Riley swung the swivel chair she was sitting in, turning her around to face the captain and everyone else.

"Tony, where did Miss Morgan live before she came here three years ago?"

Tony opened his file. "Miami."

"Whose locket did we find on Michelle?"

"Miss Morgan's."

Riley turned to his captain. "You think she doesn't know something about this murder? You said we have a killer who goes after blondes—blondes that look a lot like Michelle."

He turned and lifted the glasses off Miss Morgan's shocked face, then released her hair from its clip. An audible gasp sounded throughout the room as long blond locks cascaded around her shoulders.

"Well, what do you all think about this?"

Chapter Three

Stunned silence permeated the room.

"Riley, I want to see you in my office now." Captain Lewis's tone was soft and lethal. "O'Connor will stay with Miss Morgan."

Riley followed him into the office and tried not to notice his captain's clenched fists or the heavy rise and fall of his chest.

With a steely gaze, he pinned Riley to his seat. "You have a choice, MacIntyre—voluntary three-day bereavement leave with pay or mandatory three-day suspension without pay, and one extremely unhappy captain who will make your life a living hell. Which will it be?"

Riley groaned and scrubbed his face with his hands.

"You are not working this case. You were too close to the victim to be objective and your behavior with Miss Morgan proves that."

Riley glanced at Devra through the office window. She'd managed to pull her hair back again, completely changing the way she looked. Pat O'Connor was smiling, patting her on the shoulder, comforting her after the trauma she'd been forced to endure. Somehow, he had to make the captain see he was on to something, that he was right about her. "That woman knows a lot more about this case than she's letting on."

"Based on what?"

"My gut."

"Your gut isn't good enough, considering the circumstances."

"It's never been wrong before and you know it."

"The victim has never been part of your family before."

The image of Michelle lying on the dirty French Quarter sidewalk flashed through his mind, making his own fists clench. "That's bull."

"The truth is you've never been this unhinged before. You've always been Mr. Cool, Mr. Confident—hell, Mr. Cocky. Now you're a loose cannon and I won't have your emotions jeopardizing this case. Take your three days and spend the time with your family. Rest, relax, and when you come back, you can focus on the night stalker case and let Pat and his team handle this one with the FBI."

Somehow he didn't think "Ladies' Man Pat" would do what it took to find Michelle's killer. "I can see his charm is working wonders on *my* suspect as we speak. She's all ready to let loose and spill everything she knows any minute now." They both watched Pat through the glass. Though he was trying, Miss Morgan was sitting as stiff and tight-lipped as a pastor's wife in a Bourbon Street strip club.

"You've been known to load on the charm yourself," the captain grumbled.

Usually, Riley thought, but not when it came to her. That woman just drove the charm right out of him.

"Just stay clear from her. Got it?" The captain ordered on an exasperated sigh.

Riley nodded, but continued watching Devra out of the corner of his eye.

"By the way, your father has called three times. I'm going downstairs. You can use my office to call him back. Consider that an order."

Riley swore under his breath as the captain slammed the door behind him. Sometimes it didn't pay to have a powerful father. He wondered how much his forced leave had to do with his old man, then pushed the thought out of his head. Tony had had the same idea earlier and if it'd been anyone else, Riley would probably even agree. Anyone with a loss of this magnitude should take their three days, but the worst part was having his case ripped out from under him.

Surreptitiously, he watched Miss Morgan. Three days of mandatory leave—three days to get that woman to crack. He raked a hand through his hair. Three days to get the answers he needed for his brother, Mac, and his old man.

A lead weight dropped to the pit of his stomach as he picked up the phone and dialed the ranch. "Hey, LuAnn," he said when his stepmom answered the phone. "How's Dad?"

"Devastated like the rest of us, but he'll be glad to hear from you. Hold on, hon, and I'll get him for you."

Riley waited, not sure what to expect from his dad and not able to take his eyes off the enigma of a woman sitting at his desk. He was going to make it his priority to find out everything about her that he could and flush out whatever she was hiding from him.

He watched Tony bring her a cup of water. She nodded, thanking him, a trace of a smile touching her face. As she sipped the water, a hint of moisture wet her seductive lips. She turned, her melting blue eyes meeting his through the glass. Awareness rushed through him, hot and thick, making him cringe.

He was going to take her down.

"Hey, Son." His father's voice sounded dull through the receiver.

Riley turned away from the glass. "Hey, Dad."

"When you coming home?"

"Soon."

"Good, 'cause we all need to be here right now to support your brother. He's taking it real hard."

Guilt slithered through him. "Yeah, I suppose he is."

"He has a lot of unanswered questions. We're hoping you can fill him in."

"I don't have a lot of answers right now. If I'd known what Michelle had been planning... I didn't know she'd try to draw this guy out alone, Dad."

"We know you didn't, Son. No one blames you."

Riley knew that, but he could still hear the quiet disappointment in his old man's voice, disappointment that had been festering for eighteen years. And now he had Michelle to account for, too. A heavy weight pressed against his chest.

"Who knows what she was thinking?"

"She wanted to nail the SOB that had been cutting up women in the Quarter. Only she hadn't been prepared for a new monster...a different monster. I'm going to find her killer, Dad. I promise," he whispered, his voice raw with emotion.

"I know you will, Son. I know you won't let us down."

No, not again I won't.

Riley ground his teeth with frustration as he hung up the phone. He took a deep breath, steeling his emotions as he watched Miss Morgan talking with Pat and Tony. There she was, playing the demure little kitten again, but it wasn't as convincing without her big blue eyes directed his way. Now he could easily see through her little game. Her shifty little glances kept giving her away.

He left the office and approached them. "Come on, Miss Morgan. I'll take you home."

"Why don't you let me do that," Pat said, rising. "You go home to your family." He stood possessively over her, his chest puffing up like a peacock's.

Made Riley want to spit. "That's quite all right, Pat. Thanks for the concern and the offer." He dropped the good-ole-boy smile and pierced him with a cold stare. "Miss Morgan and I have some unfinished business. I'm sure you understand."

Pat held his gaze for a moment, then looked away.

Riley turned back to Devra. She was staring at him, her fear shining like a beacon in her luminous eyes. Yeah, she was good—he took her by the arm and led her away—but he was better.

DEVRA STARED OUT of the Expedition's window, pushing loose tendrils of hair back into their clip. Everything in its place, her mother used to say. Thankfully, the detective hadn't muttered a word since they left the station. As he stopped in front of her house, she hopped out of the car and all but ran toward her door. Dark storm clouds raced across the sky. Electricity sparked the hairs on the back of her neck. Either that, or it was the detective's close proximity as he followed behind her.

"Mind if I come in for a minute?" he asked when she stopped to unlock the door.

She turned, looking up into his dark brown eyes. They looked...*tormented.* She pushed back the compassion rising within her. "I can't imagine what else we have to say to each other."

"I have something I'd like to say."

She cringed at the plea in his voice, at the pain clearly etched in his eyes. She could feel his anguish. A part of her wanted to help him. But she couldn't. To do that, she'd have to trust him with her secrets, and trust was a luxury she couldn't afford.

She turned away from him and waited, but he didn't speak. Didn't leave. She took a deep breath, knowing it was a mistake even as the words left her mouth. "All right, but only for a minute." She'd listen, but she wouldn't help him—that would cost her too much. She opened the door and they walked in.

Inside, the house was hot and heavy with humidity, but it wasn't nearly as uncomfortable as his presence behind her. She set the ceiling fan in motion and watched the wide wooden paddles spin, circulating a gentle breeze.

The detective stood just inside her living room, studying her. She could feel his gaze on her exposed skin, hot and demanding. He made her nervous and jittery, but there was something else, too. An emptiness and longing for something she couldn't quite name. The need left her restless and shaken.

As the first drops fell, she opened the windows, letting in the thick smell of ozone as the rain battered the white petals of the gardenias outside. She loved the rain, loved the calming sensation that came over her as the water cleansed the earth, washing away the dirt and grime. "What was it you wanted to say, Detective?" she asked while watching a bird bathe in the sudden shower.

"I'd like to ask you a question."

"All right."

"What's with the getup?"

She turned to him. "I'm sorry?"

"The schoolmarm imitation?"

Stunned, she could only stare. "Is that a professional question?"

"Doesn't your hair hurt being yanked back so severely it pulls at the corners of your eyes?"

She walked toward him, refusing to let him intimidate her. She'd made it through the hard part, she'd made it past his captain. He was off the case and he was blowing off steam, acting like a petulant boy in the throws of a temper tantrum.

"Do you really need glasses? And what was with the

Poor-Little-Miss-Timid routine at the station, when we both know you're anything but?"

Her fists tightened at her sides and she glared at him. How could she have considered helping him, even for a second?

His hardened jaw eased into a cocky smile.

"You have no right to talk to me that way."

"I have every right. You know more than you're telling."

Suddenly, he was in front of her, backing her against the wall. The heat from his body scorched her skin right through the stiff cotton fabric of her dress. She gasped short breaths. Her heart pounded in her ears. He leaned down close. His cologne, rich and spicy, overwhelmed her senses.

"Stop," she murmured.

His dark eyes filled her vision and clouded her mind.

"What are you hiding?" he said softly, the rich timbre of his voice stroking sensitive nerve endings.

"Nothing."

"Why are you hiding?" he whispered and gently released her hair clip. He speared his fingers through her hair, lifting it and letting it tumble across her shoulders. His fingertips brushed against the skin on the back of her neck, sending a slow shiver tumbling down her arms.

She couldn't get enough air. His heat, his touch, his pure animal masculinity was making her weak in the knees. Her eyelids fluttered, her skin burned and a yearning deep down in the pit of her stomach made her want to scream.

"Leave me alone," she pleaded, knowing full well she didn't want him to leave her alone. She wanted him to pull her up against him, to soothe the pressure building in her aching breasts, to smother her lips with a kiss so passionate it could rip the fabric of her being.

How could I want him? She almost cried the thought out loud.

"Why was Michelle wearing your locket?" he persisted, his voice a husky whisper, his breath hot on her cheek.

She barely heard him. Her peripheral vision darkened and all she could see, all she could focus on, was his mouth. *What would he taste like?*

"Tell me why," he demanded, shaking her loose from her fervent thoughts.

"I don't know what you want from me."

"I want to know who killed Michelle," he insisted, clearly exasperated.

"I said I don't know!"

He pulled away from her and stormed out of the room. Shaken, she fell into the nearest chair. She heard the water running in the bathroom and took a deep breath. Why wouldn't he just leave her alone? She couldn't help him. She wouldn't. Lord, she was scared. She was confused, and she felt sick to her stomach. And on top of all that, she'd never been more attracted to anyone in her entire life. And he hated her. She could feel it with every breath he took.

And worse, she hated him. He was a bully, a cretin, a scourge of the earth. The very last thing she wanted was for him to touch her. She placed a hand over her fluttering heart.

The very last thing.

DAMN THAT WOMAN! She had to be the most exasperating female he'd ever met with those big blue eyes and tremulous lips. She looked tempting enough to ravish— almost. Until he reminded himself what a chameleon she was, an expert manipulator. Well, she wouldn't work her charms on him. He was on to her game.

Riley splashed cold water onto his face, then stared at his reflection in the mirror. Bloodshot eyes and a hard grimace exposed fatigue and hopelessness. He had to get hold of himself. He wouldn't get her to crack by flying off the handle. He had to be smart about this. He must get his emotions in check. He couldn't go home empty-handed. He had to have something to tell Mac and his dad. Anything. He would get this woman to talk.

In the mirror's reflection, he saw a room behind him. He stood just outside the door and listened down the hallway. All was clear. In the room, a large desk littered with papers held a sleek computer. He didn't know computers very well, but he could tell that this was one impressive setup. He walked into the room and noticed several boxes half full next to the closet door. Packing?

He approached her desk and glanced at the papers lying next to the keyboard. All double-spaced pages with the name Miller in the header. *Miller?* More pages lay facedown in the top tray of a laser jet. He picked them up, and scanned the first few lines. Alarm tightened his gut as he continued to read.

From the shadows he watched the blonde sashay down the stone tiles of St. Peter Street. Plastic gold-and-green dice bounced on her chest as her turquoise pumps clickity-clacked in rhythm with her sway.

"Hey, lady, looking good tonight. Want me to read your fortune?"

The woman glanced at the tarot card readers lining Jackson Square, then threw a cute one a wave. "No, thanks. Tonight I make my own fortune."

"I just bet you do," the man responded, laughing.

He watched their exchange, then saw her steal a glimpse behind her, searching for whoever had been following her as she'd left the Café Du Monde and headed toward Bourbon Street. His footsteps had been steady, but in the darkness, she hadn't been able to make out the source. He'd made sure she wouldn't.

She slipped her hand under her jacket and shifted the Glock in her waistband. He knew she was carrying one; what cop wouldn't when in the Quarter alone? The way she was dressed, he guessed she was trying to lure out the night stalker who'd been cutting up whores. He'd been watching her for over an hour, if anyone was helping her, he'd have known it. It was foolish of her to go it alone—foolish for her, advantageous for him. Tonight, she'd get more than she bargained for.

She turned right down Royal, heading for a more isolated street. He smiled at his good fortune. This time of night there were too many hosts standing outside trendy bars and restaurants, hoping to draw in the tourists.

His heartbeat rose in anticipation. Excitement crawled along his skin as she turned left onto Orleans Street, once again heading toward the raucous noise of Bourbon Street. Here, no one would hear her scream.

He closed in. Her quick furtive glances behind her betrayed her fear. She could feel him hunting her. He enjoyed this part of the game, perhaps even more than the kill itself. She quickened her pace. He left her.

From his new vantage point, he watched her turn again. She stopped and listened, becoming aware that his footsteps had fallen silent. She let loose a deep sigh, and the corners of her mouth lifted slightly as she shook her head. She continued up the block to Bourbon Street, toward him. People up ahead were laughing and stumbling their way down the neon alley. She visibly relaxed even more.

As she approached, he stepped out from behind an old-fashioned cast-iron lamppost. Alarm chased across her face. She reached behind her, grasping the Glock's handle.

"Hey, Michelle," he said softly and gave her a disarming smile.

She squinted into the dull light from the dirt-encrusted lamp, trying to get a handle on him. Recognition dawned. She relaxed, dropping her shoulders. "Hey. What's up?"

"What are you doing out here?"

"Just heading to Bourbon Street."

"It's not safe to be out here alone. Let me walk you."

"You know I can take care of myself." She took a quick glance behind her, then threw him a smile. "But I don't mind the company."

They'd only taken a few steps before he motioned to a doorway on the right. "What's that?"

She peered into the darkness. Before she could turn back, he seized her. His big hands wrapped around her neck, squeezing as he shoved her up against the wall. She clawed at his wrists. He could feel her heart hammering with fear. She let go of his wrists and tried to reach behind her for the Glock.

"Oh, no, you don't," he hissed.

He twisted the beads around her neck, applying more pressure, squeezing harder. Her eyes widened as she choked for air. She slumped forward. He pushed her back, grabbed the gun and pocketed it.

Breath surged back into her lungs and she gulped it. The blade flashed in the dim light from the street lamp. In one swift movement, it was over and she slid down the wall. He took something gold and shiny and slipped it around her neck. A gold heart with a rose etched across the front dangled between her breasts, nestling amidst the rivulets of blood seeping from her throat.

Riley swayed as pain and confusion obscured his vision. He stormed through the house, a burning rage pushing him beyond control. He slammed the wad of papers bunched in his hands onto the table. "I want the truth and I want it now."

Devra's eyes widened as she stared at the papers.

"You were there. You saw the whole thing. Tell me who killed her."

She stood, her chair falling behind her with a loud crash. "I wasn't there."

"Then what is this?"

"It's just a scene from my book."

"Bull. This is a reenactment of Michelle's murder."

Devra covered her face with her hands.

He gripped the table's edge to stop himself from grabbing her shoulders and giving her a good shake. "You know too many details for someone who wasn't there!"

She tried to back away from him, but hit the wall behind her. "I wasn't there. I swear."

"Liar," he roared.

She covered her ears and squeezed her eyes shut. "I'm not a liar. I didn't kill her. I swear I didn't."

He stepped closer, leaning down into her face. "I want the truth."

"I didn't." She swayed before him, her eyes glazed and frightened. "I didn't kill Tommy, Papa." The color drained from her face and she collapsed in a heap onto the floor.

Stunned, Riley dropped to his knees beside her. "Come on, lady. Wake up." He gritted his teeth to restrain himself from clutching her in his arms to make sure she was okay.

Long lashes fluttered on her cheeks. She opened luminous eyes full of hurt and vulnerability and pinned him to the wall. He felt a need to apologize, to help her in some way. Dammit, why wouldn't she just tell him the truth?

"What happened?" she asked with a shaky voice.

"You fainted," he muttered, and tried to swallow his irritation.

She sat up, cradling her head in her hands. "I'm sorry. Really, I am. I know you want answers, and I wish I had them for you. But I don't. I just don't."

Tears filled her eyes, and damn if they didn't work. He could feel the fury seeping right out of him. Apparently, he was in worse shape than he thought. He needed sleep. He needed food. He needed to go home, recoup and try to sort this mess out again later.

"Listen—"

The sound of crashing glass reverberated through the room. Riley jumped to his feet as splintered shards scattered across the floor. Clumps of glass mixed with something red hit the sides of the sofa and oozed down the fabric. Devra let out a bloodcurdling scream, shattering Riley's ragged nerves.

He turned back to her. "It's okay," he said, then bent

down and touched the wet squishy substance. *Raspberries?* "What the hell?" Pulverized red berries covered the hardwood floor at Devra's feet. Riley looked at her, at once concerned by the blank stare and chalky color of her skin. "It's only berries," he said, trying to assure her. "Raspberries."

She started to rock, emitting a strange moaning sound. Riley watched, a wave of hopelessness crashing over him. There was nothing fake about her pain. Obviously, something bad had happened to her in her past.

Something he didn't want to deal with.

"I'm sure it was just a prank. I'll show you," he said and dashed out the front door, expecting to find a couple of giggling boys hightailing it down the block, but the street was deserted. Back inside, Devra was still on the floor, holding herself and rocking back and forth. He placed a hand on her shoulder.

She looked up and met his eyes. Her face was red, wet and swollen, but that didn't bother him as much as the anguish he saw in her eyes. And the fear. Genuine grab-you-by-the-balls-and-squeeze kind of fear.

This was no game.

"Talk to me," he pleaded, kneeling down next to her.

For an eternal moment, she just stared at him, unblinking and barely breathing. Then she gulped a breath and grabbed the front of his shirt with both hands.

"He's back!"

Chapter Four

"Who?" Riley asked, at once filled with hope that they were finally getting somewhere. "Who is *he?*"

She released his shirt and dropped her gaze to the floor. "I don't know."

Riley blew out a frustrated sigh. He didn't have time for this, not the patience nor the energy.

"You don't understand," she said, her eyes beseeching him to do just that. "Everyone thought it was me, and sometimes I believed it myself. But deep down, I knew it couldn't have been me. No matter what they all thought, they were wrong. The locket proves that." She stood and gestured toward the gooey mess on the floor. "So does this."

Riley needed a shower to clear the grit out of his eyes and a pot of strong coffee for the cobwebs in his head. Then, and only then, would he have a minuscule chance of figuring out what in the hell she was babbling about. "Can we just slow this boat down, back up and try again?" He held up the typed pages. "Let's start with these."

She stared at the papers. "Yes, those. Well…"

He waited for an eternity. "I'm drowning here."

She looked him in the eye and stated matter-of-factly, "I have dreams."

He took another deep breath and slowly let it out before responding, "Yes, don't we all."

"No, I mean I have *dreams*." Her big blue eyes locked onto his as she emphasized the word.

"The water's real muddy over here. I'm not following."

She took the papers from his hand and held them up. "I had this dream last night."

He looked from her, to the papers, then back to her again.

"It's true," she insisted.

"You expect me to believe you dreamed Michelle's death in precise detail, then typed it all down?"

"Yes."

He'd heard of cases like this. Who hadn't? Every other shop in the Quarter spouted a voodoo priestess, palm reader or some other psychic brouhaha. New Orleans was a mecca for paranormal nutcases. He'd never put much stock in them before and he certainly wasn't hearing anything that would convince him to now. He shook his head. "I don't know where to go with this. Your story's a little over the top, even for New Orleans. Let's stick with the facts."

"How could I have given Michelle my locket if I didn't even have it?" she insisted.

"How can I be sure you didn't?"

Her eyes rolled heavenward. "Because Joey, the little boy at the hospital, gave it to a man claiming to be my friend. I told you this already."

"We're still checking on that." He made a mental note to call Tony and have him talk to Joey and the nurse.

"Then there's this." Again, she gestured toward the mess on the floor.

"It's some kids' idea of a prank," he countered.

"No, it's not," she insisted. "Raspberries were Tommy's favorite fruit. Whoever did this knew that. Whoever did this knew about Tommy."

Riley groaned in exasperation. "Who the hell is Tommy?"

"Tommy is the boy I didn't kill!"

Riley dropped his head and gave it a shake. This just kept getting better and better.

DEVRA COULD TELL he didn't believe a word she said. Doubt and suspicion were all he could see, all he could feel. Why had she thought he'd be any different than the others? To this day, the whole town of Rosemont, Washington, population twelve hundred and fifty-four, still believed she killed Tommy Marshall, including her own parents.

"Fine, don't believe me, but believe this," she said. "This thing, whatever *it* is, is escalating."

Riley looked up at her, exhaustion turning his eyes as murky as the Mississippi. "How's that?"

"This time, something of mine was taken. This time, the killer has made direct contact by smashing my window. That has never happened before. Somehow,

Michelle's killer has learned about me." *Michelle's killer.* Her stomach clenched as she said the words. He wasn't just Michelle's killer; he'd killed all the poor women she'd dreamed about over the years.

And now he was after her.

Why else had he taken her locket? Why else had he led the police to her? He must have been following her, watching her, and when he saw the locket drop, took it.

"Before?" The detective's voice broke. "What do you mean that hasn't happened before?"

She stared at him. Should she tell him about the others? If she did, would he protect her or would he assume she'd left a string of victims across the nation and take her in? She wished she knew if she could trust him. Just once, she wished someone would look into her eyes and believe she wasn't capable of murder.

She spotted the rock and the plastic net that had held the berries in place. She pointed to the items. "If this was just a prank done by a couple of kids, why didn't they just throw the rock? This was personal. The addition of the berries proves it. He's playing a game, trying to scare me. Can't you see that?"

Felix strolled into the room, turned his nose up at the mess and immediately started rubbing himself against Riley's legs.

"I have to leave," she said, staring at the cat and biting down on her lower lip to keep it from trembling. "I can't stay here any longer. It's not safe. It's obvious he's been following me."

"You can't run. Running doesn't solve anything. Let me help you. Tell me who he is."

She looked into the detective's dark brown eyes for any sign of sincerity, but she just couldn't find it. He didn't want to help her. No one did.

"I don't know who he is," she insisted.

He rubbed his face with his hands, but the fatigue remained clearly etched in the lines around his eyes. "Do you have any friends or family in the area you can stay with?"

She shook her head.

"If you're right and the killer has been following you, chances are you'll be his next target. Unfortunately, I can't let you leave the area. I still have too many questions, especially about these." He gestured toward the pages once more. "It's against policy, but considering the circumstances I'm going to make an exception and let you come home with me. No one will be able to find you there."

Devra stared at him. Had she heard him right? "I couldn't."

He shrugged. "Either way, you know more about this case than you've let on and these papers prove it. I won't let you out of my sight until I get answers I can accept about how you're connected to Michelle's murder."

"But I can't stay with *you*," she croaked.

"Suit yourself. But if you really believe you're in danger, what choice do you have? And what better place to be than under the watchful eye of one of NOPD's finest?"

Devra thought she'd be ill. She couldn't spend another minute with this man, let alone a whole night.

"And besides," he continued smugly. "You're under orders not to leave town."

"Whose?"

"Mine."

This couldn't be happening to her. But he was right. What choice did she have? "I'll stay at a hotel."

"With this monster cat?"

"I'll stay at a pet hotel."

"All right, but have you actually ever been in one of those places?" He scratched his arms as a look of disgust crossed his face.

Devra would have laughed if her situation weren't so desperate.

"Bring the cat to my ranch. You'll both love it there. Unless you prefer fleas for roommates."

That was a tough one.

"If it will make you feel any better, my parents live at the ranch, too. Along with my brother and Mich—"

Pain flashed through his eyes. No, Michelle didn't live there anymore. Maybe he did believe she was in danger. If he really thought she was a killer, would he bring her into his home? Maybe, just maybe there was a chance he would help her. She thought she had him pegged as a self-absorbed egomaniac, but perhaps…

Nah, she was kidding herself. He just wanted her close to keep an eye on her. But he had a point—how much safer could she be than under his protection? She looked at her shattered window and the mess around her living room, then let out a reluctant sigh. She certainly couldn't spend another night here. Not now. Not ever again. "All right, you win."

"Good, then it's all settled." He gave her a smile—wide, devastatingly charming and beaming with triumph.

Lord, what had she gotten herself into now?

"TONY," RILEY SAID quietly into his cell phone as he stepped onto Devra's front porch.

"Riley, where are you?"

"Miss Morgan's house."

"Still? Are you crazy? The captain made it clear Pat's working the Morgan angle and we're to go back to the night stalker case. He said you have three days' leave."

"Yeah, forced leave," Riley muttered.

"So, what are you still doing there? Or have you grown tired of being a cop and want to throw your career away?"

"Never, buddy. I've convinced Miss Morgan to come stay at the ranch with me for a few days."

"What? Are you nuts?"

"Oh, and you don't know where she is."

"You better believe I don't. You're diggin' yourself in deep. Just keep me out of it. Don't tell me another word 'cause I don't want to know."

"Would, bro, except I need your help."

"No way. You're on your own on this one."

"Tony, she knows things about Michelle's murder she shouldn't. She's also mentioned the death of someone named Tommy, but I haven't got the specifics on that one yet. She has a lot to answer for and, I suspect, a lot more she's hiding. I'm going to get the truth out of her, even if I have to turn on the MacIntyre charm and hit her with both barrels."

Tony snorted. "What are you going to do when your old man finds out his dinner guest is a suspect in his daughter-in-law's murder?"

"I wouldn't take her home if I thought she was Michelle's killer."

Tony paused. "Then what do you think she's hiding?"

"I have no idea, but she's the key to this case. I can feel it in my gut."

"You're making a big mistake."

"Maybe. In any case, I need you."

"No way."

"Please, I'm beggin' here. Do it for Michelle."

"Oh, great, bring out the guilt artillery."

"I'm down on one knee."

"All right, all right. What is it already? What do you want me to do?"

"Some punk threw a rock through Miss Morgan's window. Can you bag it and check for prints?"

"A rock?"

"Yeah, and berries. It's a real mess."

"Berries? That's plain dumbass weird."

"Tell me. I'm sure it's nothing, but the lady insists it isn't, so let's give her the benefit of the doubt."

"All right. I'll do it."

"Thanks. Also, can you drop by the hospital and talk to a kid named Joey who was in Miss Morgan's story time this morning? And a cute nurse named Betty Jenkins. Apparently, some guy was watching Miss Morgan read to the kids last week. This kid, Joey, found her locket and gave it to him. Maybe we can get a sketch artist to work with them."

"Sounds good. I'll pass the information on to Pat."

"All right," Riley agreed reluctantly. "Hey, why don't you join us for dinner tonight?"

"No way. You need to be alone with your family. Besides, I'm sure they'll have a lot of questions and I don't have any answers."

Riley cringed. "You and me both."

"You can't avoid them forever. Having me or even Miss Morgan around isn't going to stop them from wanting to know what happened."

"I know."

There was a heavy pause before Tony added, "It wasn't your fault. There wasn't anything you could have done."

Wasn't there? "I could have kept a better eye on her. Mac depended on me for that."

"An eye on Michelle? Like I told you before, she had a mind of her own and once she got it wrapped around something, there was no stopping her and you know it. Better yet, Mac knows it, too."

Riley blew out a deep breath. "I know you're right, but it isn't going to make seeing Mac again any easier."

DEVRA'S STOMACH twisted into knots as she threw her clothes into an overnight bag. How could she have agreed to go home with Detective MacIntyre? How could she spend day and night with the man knowing every moment he'd be probing her mind, trying to get her to slip up? Still, what choice did she have? Until the killer was caught, she'd spend the rest of her life looking over her shoulder, wondering who he was and when he'd strike next. Her best bet was for the police to find him and for them to do it without involving her.

Not that they'd ever been able to before. But maybe on this ranch, she could disappear. She doubted the detective told anyone what he was doing. His captain wanted him out of the picture. Perhaps she could use that to her advantage. She met him out front, handed him her bag and the cat carrier, then climbed into the Expedition. "Have you told anyone I am staying with you?"

Speculation shone in his eyes as he looked at her.

She didn't say anything, just waited for him to respond. Sometimes silence was the best answer.

"Just my family."

"What have you told them about me?" she asked, trying to sound as casual as possible.

"Not much, just that you need my help for a few days."

"Is that all the time you think it will take to find this guy?"

"That's all the time I believe we'll need to get to the bottom of who broke your window."

She ignored the prick of disappointment. He still didn't believe her. How could he protect her if he didn't believe she was in danger? She rested her head against the seat and stared out the window, barely noticing as freeway gave way to large green expanses dotted with houses as they drove farther and farther away from the city.

A few days. She probably shouldn't stay longer than that anyhow. Somehow, this killer from her dreams always managed to find her. But how? A rush of goose bumps swept down her arms. She almost hoped he would find her at this cop's ranch and she hoped the detective would be waiting for him with a big black gun. Maybe then she would find a moment of peace.

The rain diminished to a slow sprinkle that quickly evaporated to thicken the heavy air. Soft Dixieland jazz played on the radio, soothing her tortured nerves. Her gaze followed the rolling mound that led to the levy before shifting to the sideview mirror. A gray Honda followed closely behind them. There was only one person in the car—a man.

She glanced at the handsome detective out of the corner of her eye, but he didn't seem to notice the Honda. Would she be able to depend on him? No, she'd never been able to depend on anyone. If she wanted this killer stopped, she'd have to find a way to do it herself.

"How's Felix doing?" Riley asked, breaking into her thoughts.

"Good. He's a great traveler," she answered, but kept her eyes on the sideview mirror. "Thanks for letting him come. I wouldn't have been able to sleep without him."

"Never been apart, huh?"

"No. He's been my only family for a long time now."

The detective looked at her with questions filling his eyes. But she didn't give him any answers. That's what the next few days would be like—him probing, her evading. They continued down the road in silence, his eyes on the road in front of them, hers focused on the car behind them. At last, the Honda turned off onto a side road and disappeared from view. Tension seeped out of her.

"Your cat is going to love the ranch," Riley said. "We have six horses, four dogs, at least three cats and a few ducks."

Devra looked at him, her eyes wide. Just where was he taking her?

"My stepmother, LuAnn, trains horses and I'm afraid she has a soft spot for abandoned animals. She takes them in, heals them, loves them until they're happy and healthy, then tries to find homes for them. More often than not, she gets so attached she can't bear to part with them."

"She sounds like a very special woman."

"She has a huge heart beneath a tough exterior. Mac and I tried everything we could think of to make her life miserable after she married my dad. She never held it against us. Not even after the snake episode."

Devra's heart skipped a beat. "I'm not sure I want to hear about the snake episode."

He smiled and as much as she didn't want to, she found herself smiling back at him. Another one of his tactics, she was sure.

A few minutes later, they turned right onto a gravel road and drove under a large cast-iron arch that spelled out the word MacIntyres. A huge antebellum home sat back from the road amidst a cluster of guardian live oaks that had to be at least two hundred years old.

Devra stared at the house, awestruck by the towering columns and wraparound verandah. "I thought you said you lived on a ranch?"

"I do. This is it."

"Looks more like Tara to me," she muttered. "You actually live here?"

"Yep. Grew up here, as did my daddy and his daddy before him."

"Incredible. I'm afraid Felix and I will probably get lost."

"Don't worry. You'll be staying with me. I have a much smaller place in back."

Devra wasn't sure what she'd expected, but it wasn't a Southern mansion and it certainly wasn't staying in "something smaller out back" with just him. They continued around a barn-shaped five-car garage to a small farmhouse hidden behind a cluster of trees. She couldn't take her eyes off the old-fashioned front porch offering two inviting granny rockers.

He parked in front of a massive live oak shading the walk. "This is it."

"It's beautiful," she said, taken in by the peaceful setting.

"Wait 'til you see the river behind the house. Do you like to fish?"

Devra turned to him. "I don't know. I've never been."

His mouth twisted into a smirk. "That is a sin against nature. What have you been doin' all your life?"

"Not much." She was embarrassed to admit it. That's what happened when you lived in fear of people finding out who you were, what you'd done and where you'd been.

"You had better change that. Life's too short to let it pass you by without enjoying all she has to offer, and fishing is most definitely near the top of life's most enjoyable experiences."

He was actually smiling at her. "Near?" she asked distracted by the humor brightening his face. It was having a strange effect on her, lifting her spirits and the corners of her mouth. She wasn't at all sure she liked it.

"Oh, yeah. You don't need me to tell you what's at the top, do you?" His suggestive gaze swept her body, lighting a flame deep in her belly.

Heat suffused her cheeks. She just kept stepping in it, didn't she?

He chuckled and leaped out of the truck. "Come on, let's settle the cat so we can get some supper."

"Sounds good to me," she said, realizing how hungry she was. And maybe if her mouth was full of food, she'd stop sticking her foot in it.

RILEY TOOK HIS TIME settling his guest in his house. He wasn't ready to face his family, to see the disappointment and questions lingering in their eyes. He led Miss Morgan through the grounds, pointing out the names of the lush vegetation as they slowly followed the river path toward the back door of the estate.

She had changed into a cream-colored dress that glided like silk over her soft curves as she walked. He tried not to notice, tried to ignore the subtle scent of vanilla he caught a whiff of every now and again. But she kept drawing him back with her small sweet smile and sultry voice. As they approached the house, he wished he could slip his arm around her waist and turn her in another direction. He wished he were anywhere but home.

"Is everything all right?" she asked, and he realized they were standing outside the back door.

Nothing would ever be all right unless they found Michelle's killer. He wanted to continue walking down the path, but he had to go in and face his family. Unease tightened his stomach as he stood staring at the back door.

Concern entered her expressive eyes.

"Everything's fine," he assured her and opened the door. The heavy floral scent assaulted him the second they walked into the kitchen. Every spare inch of counter space was covered with flowers, casseroles and every dessert known to the South. News spread fast in this small Southern community. Especially bad news.

"Let's leave this door open. I can hardly breathe in here," he said and propped open the door.

She nodded and straightened her dress, her fingers fluttering as she patted her hair.

Suddenly, he could easily see her beauty hiding behind her glasses and tightly pulled back hair. She wasn't fooling anyone. "You'll be fine. They won't bite," he assured her.

"I'm…just not used to meeting new people. Even under the best of circumstances, which this obviously isn't." She gestured toward the flowers.

She was right. This wasn't the best time to spring her on the folks. "It will be okay, you'll see." Besides, there wasn't anything he could do about it now. He couldn't send her back to his house alone. "Anybody home?" he yelled.

"Riley." His stepmother, LuAnn, bustled into the kitchen and enveloped him in a big hug. Her swollen and puffy eyes squeezed the guilt burdening his heart. "How are you?" she asked, her sharp gaze probing his face. He nodded, not knowing what he could say.

"Your father's in his study," she said. "Dinner will just take a few minutes." She noticed Devra and took a step back, disapproval flashing through her eyes.

Riley stepped closer to Devra and placed a comforting hand on the small of her back. "LuAnn, I'd like you to meet Miss Devra Morgan. This is the woman I told you about. She'll be staying with me for a few days."

LuAnn offered her hand, but didn't mask the troubled look on her face. "It's nice to meet you, Miss Morgan. I'm sorry that we can't give you our usual warm welcome, but I'm sure you understand given our situation."

"Yes, of course," Devra responded, looking more uncomfortable than ever. "And, please, call me Devra. Both of you," she said with a pointed gaze that met and held his.

"Where's Mac?" Riley asked, though he was having a hard time breaking her eye contact.

"He took the dogs and went for a ride. He said not to wait on dinner for him. He wanted to be alone." She opened a cabinet and started removing serving platters. "He's having a hard time."

"I know," Riley said and wished he could disappear,

too. But he was thankful for the reprieve. He wasn't ready to face the condemnation he knew he'd find burning in his brother's eyes. "Look, LuAnn, it's been a real tough day. Would you mind if Miss—" Devra's raised eyebrows stopped him. "If Devra and I just took a couple plates to go?"

"No, not at all. Of course I understand. Please, go see your dad while I get it together for you."

He nodded and kissed her cheek. "Thanks, you're the best."

He wasn't sure what to expect as he entered his father's study. Usually in times of crisis his dad became stronger, more in charge, a solid leader who would support anyone who needed it. Not today. The weary face that greeted him from behind the big mahogany desk looked ragged and reminded him of the night his mother had been killed. He cut off the painful memory before it could dig in and take hold.

"How are you doing, Dad?" he asked, knowing it was a dumb question even as the words left his mouth.

"As well as can be expected, Son," his father replied. "You have news for us? Anything that will help explain how this has happened to our family?" *Again?* The unspoken word hung heavily in the air.

"Not yet. We're working on it."

"I understand you brought a young lady home with you. Timing's not real good for that, Riley."

"Trust me, Dad. I've got my reasons."

"I hope so, Son." His father let out an uncustomary sigh, his head bent as he stared at the top of his desk.

"She'll stay out of your way," Riley added, and was

thankful he and Devra would be dining alone. His family didn't need a vision of Michelle sitting across the dinner table tonight. They were too raw, too hurt. For a second, he regretted bringing her, but she'd stay until he got what he needed out of her. Until he got the truth.

Chapter Five

"So, Devra," LuAnn said as soon as Riley disappeared down the hall. "Tell me a little bit about yourself. I don't detect a Southern accent. Where are you from?"

There was something in the woman's hawk-eyed gaze that made Devra uncomfortable. "All over I guess." She offered a small smile and tried not to choke on the cloying scent of too many flowers. A pinprick of a headache started pinching her temples.

LuAnn was still staring at her. "There's something familiar about you." Her eyes squinted in speculation.

"Can I do anything to help prepare dinner?" Devra asked, and brushed her hand across her hair to make sure it was all still firmly in place.

"No. The neighbors brought enough food to feed us for a week." LuAnn turned to the fridge, removed several Tupperware containers and placed them in a bag.

Before she had a chance to question her some more, Devra turned toward the door. "Thank you so much for your hospitality. If you don't mind, I'd like to take a short walk outside."

LuAnn stopped and turned toward her. "Stay on the path, dear. We wouldn't want you to get lost."

Something in her voice sent a small shudder skipping down Devra's spine. Surely she didn't mean anything by that? As LuAnn turned away to busy herself with the food, Devra shook off her uneasiness and walked out the door. She was seeing danger where there wasn't any. She was perfectly safe here, safer than anywhere she'd probably ever been.

Still, she couldn't shake the feeling that something wasn't quite right as she followed the path in front of her. It meandered beautifully through large bushes of camellias and other flowering shrubs. In a perfect picture-postcard setting, wisteria wound its way around tree trunks forming a canopy over her head as she continued away from the house. A hummingbird flitted past her ear. She ducked and hoped it was a hummingbird, and not some giant-size insect.

The parklike setting of the estate was breathtaking. Obviously, someone had put a lot of love and care into these grounds. She should feel soothed, calm even. Yet as she walked farther down the path, the uncanny feeling that someone was watching came over her. Uneasiness prickled the nape of her neck. She stopped and turned, her gaze searching the shrubbery, but no one was there.

Obviously, her nerves were stretched too thin, she told herself. Still, she continued forward again, her ears straining for any unusual sounds. Was it possible the killer had followed them? Was there a chance he knew where she was? Something small lying farther along on the path caught her eye. She felt herself being pulled toward it, even though in the deep recesses of her mind something urged her to turn…to run.

Slowly, she approached, telling herself how silly she was, how ridiculous. Her heart started pounding, and as she stared down at the perfect yellow daisy lying in the middle of the path, she realized she couldn't move, she couldn't swallow. Images flashed through her mind—Tommy placing a yellow daisy behind her ear, ice-cold water tumbling over the rocks. She heard laughter—hers, his. Then she saw him, crumpling before her, his blood splattering her blouse. A guttural cry emitted from her chest and she dropped to her knees. The pain of the rocks pushing into her skin pushed back the long-buried memories and brought her reeling back to the present. She picked up the daisy, to prove to herself it couldn't hurt her, that it was just a flower, then wiped its soft petals across a tear on her cheek. It was a coincidence, that was all. Yellow daisies are common, they're found everywhere. She peered through the dense greenery. *Just not here.*

The slight crackle of leaves broke into her thoughts. She listened intently. There it was again. A footstep? A fist of fear clutched her heart and squeezed. "Is anyone there?" she tried to call, but her voice came out no louder than a hoarse whisper.

Silence answered her. Complete silence. There was no sound at all. Not even the raucous noise of insects or the chirping of birds. Something was wrong. "Hello," she called again, a slight quiver to her voice drawing out the syllables.

Bushes rattled behind her. She stood, turning, her breath catching in her throat, her mouth opening to scream. A bird burst through the leaves and flew into the sky. Shocked, she stared at it, then took a deep breath and tried to settle her nerves. *Only a bird.*

"Hey, there you are," Riley said as he turned a corner in the path. "You hungry?" He held up the bag of food LuAnn had packed.

She nodded and tried to school her expression so he wouldn't see her fear. There had been no one there, she told herself. She'd let her imagination run away with her. He was giving her an odd look, staring at her with speculation lighting his eyes. She tried to smile, but couldn't shake the tingling at the back of her neck or the sensation that someone was watching her.

"Is everything all right?" Riley asked.

"Yes," she said and stopped herself from taking another look over her shoulder.

"What's that you've got?" He gestured toward her hand. She held up the daisy, clutched too tightly in her grasp.

"Just a flower I found on the path. A gardener must have dropped it."

Riley frowned, his look setting her teeth on edge.

"What is it?"

"I don't recall seeing daisies on the estate."

His words brought fear surging back through her veins. The flower slipped through her fingers as a tremor rushed through her. He picked up the flower, then stared at it for a moment.

"I bet it fell out of one of LuAnn's arrangements."

"That must be it," Devra said and viciously rubbed the chill out of her arms. Keep moving, she thought. Don't let him see your fear.

They continued down the river path, walking in silence. She used all her inner strength to try to pull herself together. Coincidences happen all the time, she thought. Of course LuAnn's bouquets had daisies in them—perfect, beautiful, yellow daisies. With shaky fingers, she picked a star jasmine blossom as she passed a massive vine and inhaled its sweet scent.

"Why'd you leave the house?" Riley asked. "Did LuAnn say something to upset you?"

She looked up. "No, of course not. She seems like a very nice woman. I just needed air. I'm sure your family is lovely."

His eyes caught hers, sending a fluttery heat through her tense muscles. "They are nice. And very important to me. I'll do anything for them."

Even railroad an innocent woman? Unbidden, the thought sliced through her. Even if she had managed to get away from a killer, what exactly had she gotten herself into instead?

A twig broke behind them. She gasped and turned as fear careened through her chest. Someone *is* out there—watching.

He followed her gaze. "What is it?"

She scanned the trees and bushes for any sign of movement. "Just jumpy, I guess." She let out a shaky breath and turned back to him. He was big and strong enough to protect her. She would be okay as long as he stayed with her. But would he?

"Don't worry," he said, apparently reading her thoughts. "You're perfectly safe here. No one knows where you are."

She looked into his dark brown eyes and wished she could believe him, wished she could trust him. But every time she looked at him like this, his gaze seemed to do something to her senses. It knocked her off-kilter and made her feel self-conscious, like she couldn't rely on her instincts.

"I can't shake the feeling that someone is watching me," she admitted, feeling slightly foolish.

He took her hand and gave it a squeeze, sending a jolt coursing through her. "You're going to have to trust me to do my job. We'll get to the bottom of your mystery man at the hospital and whether or not he was the one who broke your window."

Dismayed by the warmth seeping through her, she pulled her hand away. "And if he murdered Michelle."

"Exactly."

Fatigue filled her and, for a moment, she ached to lean into his strong chest and let it all go. Let someone else take care of her for a change.

Luckily, Riley turned and continued down the path. Longing for something he could never give her ballooned inside Devra as she watched him walk away. She shook off her disappointment and followed him. She needed food was all. The sooner she ate and went to bed, the better. A good night's sleep would put this new situation into perspective—would put *him* into perspective. He wasn't her knight in shining armor; he was a cop who could send her away. She'd do well not to forget that.

They were almost back at his house when she noticed a speedboat rocking gently against the dock. "Is it yours?" she asked, immediately entranced by the vessel.

"Sure is. Want to go for a ride?"

The little craft tempted her. What safer place could there be than on a boat in the middle of a river. She could almost imagine what it must feel like to have the breeze blowing her hair and her fingers trailing in the water. But she couldn't. She needed food, sleep—

"Okay," she found herself responding and wasn't at all certain where it had come from. "Maybe a boat ride is just what I need."

"Good. We can break off the main channel, go down into the swamps and catch us an alligator or two."

Her eyes widened. So much for trailing fingers. "Can't we just sit in it?"

He laughed—a warm laugh that started deep in his chest and filled the air around them. Something lurched inside her at the rich, hearty sound. Suddenly, she was noticing a lot more than long legs and a perfectly molded chest. More than boyish charm and a casual curl to his hair. There was the way his eyes, when warm, turned her insides to goo. And a hearty dose of sincerity, in a man that could be quite dangerous.

"Then again, maybe not. I should unpack," she said on a rush of air. She should be alone, safe and secure in the confines of her room. Away from these manicured, lush grounds that could hide anything and away from this handsome, laughing man who was suddenly muddling her thoughts and senses.

"Hello, brother." A large dark-haired, dark-eyed man appeared from behind a clump of trees.

Riley's laugh died on his lips.

"Who's the little filly you brought home this time?" The man edged closer, looking her up and down.

Not liking him on sight, Devra stiffened. There was something dangerous about him, *something off*.

Thick eyebrows formed a menacing scowl as if he didn't like what he saw. "And didn't you pick a hell of a fine time to do it."

Riley stepped between them, blocking her. "Mac…" He opened his arms in a gesture of peace. "Come on, buddy. I know you're hurting, but leave the lady alone."

"She's not like the usual fare you bring round," Mac said, stepping round him, his lips pulled up in a sneer.

Devra didn't like the way he was looking at her, didn't like the smell of whiskey on his breath.

"Come on, let me take you home." Riley stepped cautiously forward.

"I didn't know you liked them so plain," Mac jeered. As he moved closer, his expression twisted with confusion. He stared at her, his eyes widening, then he lunged forward and grabbed her arm. His strong fingers dug into her skin. She cried out and tried to jerk free from his grasp, but he was too strong.

"Dammit, Mac. What do you think you're doing?"

Mac pulled the glasses off Devra's face.

With all her strength, she pushed against his chest. "Get away from me." Her clip loosened, her hair falling free.

Knocked off balance, Mac floundered, then hit the

ground. He stared up at her, speechless with astonishment. "What the hell kind of sick joke is this?"

Riley took her hand and pulled her close to him. His warmth seeped into her skin, soothing her frayed nerves. She longed to lean her head against his shoulder, but knew she couldn't, knew she wouldn't be welcome.

"Are you all right?" he asked, his voice soft and comforting.

She nodded, but wasn't sure. She still felt shaken.

"I'm sorry for my brother's behavior. He's drunk, but he won't hurt you."

Skepticism twisted her mouth. "It's okay," she muttered, but it wasn't. Suddenly, she was feeling too vulnerable. If Riley looked at her with his sympathy-filled eyes one more time, she just might burst into tears. That was one thing she couldn't do. She had to stay strong. She couldn't lean on him or depend on him. She had no one to count on but herself.

"Bloody hell it's okay!" Mac yelled. "What do you think you're doing bringing a woman here today? Especially a woman that looks like…" he sputtered, gesturing wildly "…like her."

"It doesn't matter what she looks like. She's my friend and you will treat her with respect."

Devra looked up in surprise. Riley squeezed her a little tighter. "She needs my help right now and I'm not going to turn my back on her. Not for you, not for anyone."

"Isn't that sweet?" Mac sneered. "Sentiment like that coming from a man who swears he's not the protecting type, that he'd rather be the dragon than have to rescue the poor withering damsel in distress."

"She doesn't need protecting. She's quite capable of taking care of herself, as she just showed you. I don't do protection—never have, never will."

"Tell that to Michelle," Mac said with unsuppressed fury.

"I did."

Pain and anger erupted in a roar as Mac launched himself at Riley. Devra quickly stepped aside as the two men fell to the ground, tumbling one over the other.

"She was a good cop," Riley gritted between grunts. "She didn't need my protection."

"She was my wife." Mac landed a hard punch to Riley's gut. The air whooshed out of his chest as a look of pain tore across his face.

"Stop it!" Devra yelled.

Mac threw another well-placed punch, then another. "You should have watched out for her. You should have stopped this from happening."

Riley maneuvered his feet under Mac and pushed. Mac flew off him, somersaulted, then stood. Riley jumped to his feet. The two men squared off. "I couldn't stop it from happening. Don't you think I would have if I could have? I loved her, too!"

Mac grabbed Riley around the middle. They both fell, catapulting one another down the embankment and into the river.

"Stop it, please!" Devra screamed. This was too much. They were going to kill each other.

Riley stood up, soaking wet. He looked at her, then

at Mac. "I'm sorry," he muttered, and hung his head. "I had no idea…. I didn't know what Michelle was planning. I would give anything to have her back, to spare you of this."

Mac stepped closer to him, his eyes hard.

Devra inhaled a deep breath. "Please, no more," she muttered.

"I don't understand how this could have happened." Mac's voice cracked.

Riley's face contorted with pain. He put an arm around his brother and the two men fell into an awkward embrace, as Mac's body shook with grief.

Tears burned Devra's eyes. So much pain… She couldn't bear to watch any longer. She'd never had a sibling. She didn't understand the dynamics of their relationship, but to her it was too emotional…too raw.

"I'm going to check on Felix," she said to Riley as they walked out of the water.

He nodded, a look of gratitude filling his red-rimmed eyes. He squeezed her shoulder as they passed her. She watched them disappear around the bend, both soaking wet, but neither caring. Once again, she yearned to know what it felt like to have a sibling—to have someone around who loves you and looks out for you.

Suddenly, why she was there became crystal clear. *He'd rather be the dragon.* Riley would do anything he could to help his brother, even if it meant defying his captain's orders to take time off. He couldn't go near the case, so he brought the case home with him. He brought *her* home with him. He wasn't her friend. He wasn't interested in helping her or protecting her. He just wanted the truth. No matter what the cost.

The sudden knowledge made her feel more alone, more at risk than ever before. She picked up the bag of food and continued down the path toward Riley's house. Tomorrow, she would have to find a way out of this situation. She'd been a fool to think he could help her, to hope for even a moment that she wasn't in this fight alone.

She ate dinner and cleaned up the dishes, then walked slowly through the small house. His bedroom and office were on one side of the living room and kitchen, the guest room and bath on the other.

A jewel-framed snapshot on the mantel in the living room caught her attention. A pretty redhead was smiling wide with her arms wrapped around the shoulders of two little boys. The younger one had a huge happy smile and sparkling dark eyes. The other wore a gloomy rebellious look on his face. She knew instantly the boy was Riley. Time hadn't changed much.

"Come on, Felix," she announced. "Let's go feed you." She led him into the kitchen and opened a can of tuna. "See, this place isn't so bad," she cooed while stroking his back. She heard a ruckus, looked out the French doors beyond the kitchen table and saw a pack of dogs running through the yard. They were huge and loud, and there were four of them. Wide-eyed, Devra watched as the dogs cut a wide swath through the yard before disappearing around the barn. "I think we'll be keeping you inside," she said to the cat and patted him on the head.

As twilight gave way to darkness, she settled on the couch to watch TV. She must have dozed for when she opened her eyes, Michelle's face flashed across the screen, the lead story on the ten o'clock news. The newscaster announced that a local policewoman had been found murdered in the Quarter.

Devra switched off the set. She didn't want to think about Michelle's death. She didn't want to think about anything. She turned out the lights, then stood in front of the window, taking in the dark silhouette of the trees. Could someone be out there watching her?

As she stared into the darkness, a flicker of uneasiness made her squirm. She was safe here, she assured herself. As Riley said, no one knew where she was. She didn't even know where she was. She turned from the window, flicked on the porch light for Riley, then took Felix with her into the guest room.

The four-poster bed called to her. As she pulled back the sheets, she glanced out the window at the barn. Large stable lights chased away the darkness and offered small comfort. She closed the drapes, then fell into bed, exhausted.

But as tired as she was, she couldn't sleep. She lay there, listening to the moans and groans of the house, wondering what Riley was doing and when he'd be back. She beat her pillow, then rolled over. She heard a soft click. Was that the front door? She sat up, listening intently, but didn't hear another sound. What was she doing trying to sleep in a strange man's house? A man she'd just met. A man she couldn't trust.

Riley wanted answers. But if she told him what she

knew, he'd lock her up and never look back. She couldn't go through that again—the aching emptiness, the pain of abandonment. In a deep corner of her mind, she could still hear the heavy thud of a steel door closing and the suspicious, hate-filled gray eyes staring at her through the small square of glass.

"It wasn't me!" she had cried. But no one had believed her. No one had cared. A small tear wet her cheek as she closed her eyes and drifted to sleep.

IT WAS WELL PAST midnight when a gust of wind shook the bushes surrounding the house. Riley walked through his front door. The night had been incredibly hard. His family had all wanted answers, someone to blame, a reason why they were being dragged through hell. He had nothing to offer them.

His inability to help gnawed at him. He poured himself a stiff drink and stared out the window. He didn't have answers for them or for himself. But he was certain Devra held the key to this case. He'd have to do whatever it took to get her to open up. He stared at the closed door of her room and wondered if she was awake.

He hesitated in front of her door, one hand resting against the wood. She was skittish and he knew he had to move slowly. Pushing her would be the worst thing he could do. He'd wait 'til morning, until after he'd had a good night's sleep and was better prepared for the task. He dropped his hand, turned and headed toward his room. Tomorrow he'd find out exactly what she was hiding from him. He had to.

*ANGER, HOT AND LETHAL, seethed inside him. How dare
that cop bring her here to his house? Did he think he
wouldn't find her? Did he think he could keep her from
him? The thin branch grasped in his hand snapped.
She was his. It was time he taught this cop a lesson,
taught him how easily something precious, something
valued could be lost. He walked into the open area between the small house and the barn and smiled as the
mist enclosed him.*

*Inside the barn, the horse whinnied, its large brown
eyes widening with fear. He slipped the bridle over its
head, pulled him out of the barn and tied him to a tree.
Then he circled the small house, peering through the
darkened windows. He knew which one was hers. He'd
been watching.*

*The French doors leading into the kitchen opened
easily beneath his touch. Slowly, he moved through the
living room until he stood outside her closed door. He
paused to listen, then crept into the room.*

*The cat looked up, startled. Yellow eyes glimmered
in the narrow beam of his light before it darted through
the door. She slept fitfully, tossing and turning, her hand
clutching a corner of the pillow. So beautiful. She murmured as he reached for her cheek. She turned her head
away from him.*

"Peekaboo, Devra."

*She didn't wake. That was okay. It wasn't time yet;
she wasn't where he wanted her to be. He left her, taking his time as he walked through the living room,
touching, his long fingers lingering. The door to the
cop's room was opened wide. Moonlight seeped in from*

the window, betraying a mound beneath the blankets
where the arrogant cop lay sleeping.

His knife flashed in the dim light, moving closer....

SCREAMS ERUPTED through the house. Riley bolted upright, his heart pounding, his head thundering. Tangled in the blankets, he almost fell out of bed. Finding his footing, he ran to Devra's room. "What is it?" he demanded as he burst through the doorway. "What happened?"

In the middle of the bed, Devra sat with her arms clutching her knees against her chest. "Someone's in the house," she said in a hoarse whisper.

"Don't move." He checked her bathroom, her closet, then did a quick sweep of the house. There was no one. No sign that anyone had been there. He hurried back to her room. "It's okay," he assured her. "No one is here."

"Did you check your room?" she asked hesitantly.

Confused, he nodded. She released a deep breath and leaned back against the headboard. "I'm sorry. I guess I had another nightmare."

"It must have been some nightmare." He sat on the edge of her bed. "Are you all right? Do you need anything?"

She shook her head. "I'm fine. I'm sorry I woke you."

"You seem pretty shook up. What was it about?"

"Oh, I don't know," she hedged.

"Sometimes it helps to talk these things out," he offered. "Otherwise, you may never get back to sleep. And neither will I."

She smiled. It was an embarrassed smile, small and

unassuming. He liked it. He also liked the way her hair looked all mussed and draped over her shoulders. She looked soft and vulnerable. And desirable. The smooth and enticing curves of her breasts were clearly outlined through her yellow T-shirt. He forced his gaze back to her face, before his thoughts became abundantly clear through the thin cotton of his boxer shorts.

"Is it possible someone could have entered through the French doors in the kitchen?" The tone of her voice sounded soft, casual, but the sharp gleam in her eyes set him on edge.

"I'll double-check and make sure the doors are locked, though we're pretty secure out here. We close the gates at night."

Devra nodded.

"Anything else you'd like to tell me?"

She straightened the covers over her lap, refusing to meet his gaze.

"Let me help you," he said softly.

She looked up, her blue eyes locking on his. She wanted to tell him, wanted his help, he could read that need clearly on her face. If only she'd open up.

"I'm sure you were right. It was only a bad dream."

"And if I wasn't right? If it wasn't only a dream?"

For a moment she was silent, then she gave a reluctant sigh. "I dreamed someone was in the house, in this room watching me sleep." She brought her fingers to her cheek. "He touched me and said...something." Her scared gaze caught his. "I can't remember."

"It's okay," he said. "Then what happened?"

"He had a small flashlight." She looked around the

room. "He shined the light on Felix and scared him out of the room. Felix!" she called.

"He must have gone out when I came in," Riley said. "What then?"

"He went to your room." She hesitated. "He watched you sleeping." She looked up at him, a slight tinge coloring her cheeks.

She'd been dreaming about him. He felt a smile lift the corners of his mouth as he wondered exactly what his role in her dream had been.

"When I saw the knife, I woke up screaming. He was going to kill you, I know it."

Riley's smile dropped. "You don't sleepwalk, do you?"

"Not that I know of." She looked grim. "I'm sorry," she repeated.

"How about some water?"

She nodded. "That would be great, thanks."

Riley walked into the kitchen, trying to determine what it was about her story that was nagging at him, or, better yet, what about her story didn't bother him. Felix was sitting in front of the French doors staring out into the night. Riley stood behind him, trying to pinpoint what had the cat so captivated, but couldn't see anything out of the ordinary.

He turned the bolt on the door, locking it. "Come on, big guy." He picked up Felix, grabbed a bottle of water out of the fridge and returned to Devra's room.

"Felix!" she called and reached for the cat. "Thank you," she said softly.

"You're welcome. I think he wanted out, but it isn't

safe for cats out there at night. Are you going to be okay?"

She nodded, offering him another sleepy smile.

"Then go back to sleep and no more dreams," he ordered. He shut her door and was back in bed and halfway to sleep before he realized what had been nagging him. He hadn't let Felix out of her room. Her door had already been open when he'd arrived.

Chapter Six

Riley's hands stroked her hair. His index finger blazed a trail across her lips, down the column of her neck to rest in the hollow of her throat. He was looking at her, those rich brown eyes boring a hole right through her and awakening sensations that had been dormant for most of her life.

Then he kissed her.

It was warm, lingering, soft.

He touched her.

As she'd never been touched before.

He whispered her name. "Devra."

Hot fire ran like molten lava through her veins. She twined her arms around his neck pulling him down. "Oh, Riley," she whispered.

He stiffened.

She opened her eyes, but it wasn't Riley staring back at her, it was Tommy.

She gasped.

His eyes rolled into the back of his head. She felt something wet and sticky and looked down. Blood. So much blood.

She tried to scream, but it caught in her throat, choking her. He fell forward onto her, his heavy weight pushing her down. Cold water rushed over her face and ran into her mouth, filling her lungs.

She couldn't breathe.

A strange peacefulness seeped through her. She no longer felt the cold, she just felt tired. She looked up through the rushing water at the tall dark figure coming toward her.

Riley.

Devra gasped and awoke.

She stared at the ceiling, her pulse racing, her breath coming in quick breaths. Oh, Lord. She'd been dreaming! She sat straight up and shuddered. Her subconscious was trying to tell her something. But what? When would Tommy stop haunting her? When could she ever have a normal life, with normal reactions? When would she ever be able to meet a man without wondering if he was an enemy? Would he hurt her?

She stood under the hot spray of the shower, trying unsuccessfully not to think about this dream that was unlike any she'd had before. While it had the lifelike clarity and same physical stimuli that her "visions" had, this was no vision.

There was no victim. *Except for her?*

But she wasn't seeing herself being killed. There was only her...and Riley. *And so much blood.*

Hers? Tommy's? Riley's?

A sliver of dread bored into her as she dressed. Were her visions changing? Was she seeing what could happen, instead of what was happening? She shook her head. Her vision of the intruder last night had been real. Her monster had been right here in this house, in this room.

How had he found her again? Riley would have been killed, if she hadn't woken. She had to get away from here, but where could she go? The killer found her so quickly this time. She was running out of options. And worse, she was running out of hope.

She walked into the kitchen.

"Good, you're up," Riley said and pulled a mug out of the cabinet. "Sit down and have a cup of coffee. We need to talk."

She agreed.

"I think you were right," he said. "I think someone could have been in the house last night."

She took a deep gulp from her cup. *Was he starting to believe her?*

"When I came home your door had been shut, but later after you woke from your dream, I realized your door was open. Had you gotten up for any reason and perhaps left your door open?"

"No."

His dark eyes narrowed in contemplation.

She fidgeted under the scrutiny.

"Then your nightmare might very well have saved my life."

Surprise caught in her throat. "Then you believe me?"

"If it's true that you dreamed someone was in the house and, in fact, someone was, then it's not too far off the mark to believe that someone had also been standing over my bed with a knife in his hand. Or that he followed us when we left your house yesterday. Your safety here has been compromised."

"I agree. What can I do?"

"Be extra careful."

She nodded. "And?"

"Don't worry. I won't let it happen again."

Okay, not exactly what she expected to hear. What if he wasn't as all-powerful as he thought he was?

"I won't let you out of my sight. Nothing is going to happen to you on my watch."

Warmth crept up her throat at the thought of his full attention focused solely on her, while anxiety twisted and turned in her stomach. Now he'd start questioning her, wanting every detail of her visions—where they came from and how. If only she knew.

"Hope you're hungry," he said.

"Starved," she admitted, and wondered where the third degree was. Did he really believe her? She stared at his back, trying to figure him out. Instead, all she thought was how could someone look so sexy scrambling eggs? The strong muscles in his shoulders rippled as he slid the rubber spatula beneath the eggs and flipped them.

He turned, placing bowls of steaming eggs, potatoes, bacon and grits in front of her. She'd been so focused on him, she hadn't seen the abundance of food he'd prepared. "Wow," she breathed. "This is impressive."

"When you're a bachelor, you either learn to cook or starve. I don't like to go hungry."

She could see that. In fact, she was sure he didn't deprive himself of anything.

"Shouldn't we find somewhere else to stay?"

"And miss a great opportunity to catch this guy on my home turf? Not on your life."

Eyes wide, Devra looked up, a forkful of eggs midway to her mouth. But wasn't that what they were talking about? Her life? "I guess you know best," she said feeling more than a touch confused.

"Don't worry. As long as I'm around nothing will happen to you."

His confidence was not comforting. There was something about the look in his eyes that sent warning lights flashing through her mind.

A piercing scream filled the morning air. Devra dropped her fork. Riley was up and running out the door. She hesitated for only a second, then was running after him. Riley entered the barn, just as she rounded the house. She rushed forward, then slowed near the opening as she heard loud, heart-wrenching sobs that reached inside her and grabbed hold of her heart.

Tentatively, she entered the barn. LuAnn was on the ground, her face buried in the fur of one of her dogs. Both arms were opened wide and wrapped around the still bodies of two other dogs. Riley bent near the form of the fourth. Devra's throat tightened, squeezing off her breath.

"It's okay," Riley said softly. LuAnn looked up at him, her face wet and swollen. "They've been drugged, but they're not dead. Just sleeping."

"But why?" she asked. "Why would anyone do that?"

Riley looked up, catching Devra's eye. LuAnn turned to her and gave a little cry, her eyes widening with shock. "No," she moaned and shook her head.

"It's okay, LuAnn. It's only Devra. Remember, you met her yesterday."

She looked up again—eyes narrowing, lips drawing tight. "She looks so much like Michelle. I don't understand."

He went to her side and offered his hand. "I'm going to take you back to the house." He helped her stand. "The dogs are going to be all right. I'll call Dr. Williams once we get there."

She nodded and patted his hand. "Thank you, Riley." But before they'd gone two steps, she stopped and turned back to the horse stalls behind her. She left Riley's side and ran to the stalls. A deep cry escaped her.

"What is it?" Riley asked, his voice filled with anxiety.

"Storm. He's gone."

"TONY," RILEY SAID softly as his partner answered the line. "I need you to do me a favor and check with the phone company to see if any calls were placed from my house last night."

"Why, what happened?"

"We've had an intruder. LuAnn's prized stallion is missing and the dogs were drugged."

"You think Miss Morgan had something to do with it?"

"I don't know what to think."

"I think you should find the lady a nice hotel."

"Not yet. But do me a favor and see if she has a cell phone."

"Your call. She could be a total whack job. I hope you know what you're doing."

Riley couldn't get the image of someone standing over his bed wielding a knife out of his mind. What if it had been her? What if she were completely insane? He couldn't get a handle on why a serial killer who was allegedly after Devra would go after him or steal a horse. It made no sense.

"So do I, Tony."

CAUTIOUSLY, DEVRA walked farther into the barn.

Riley had taken LuAnn back to his house to call the veterinarian. She was all alone, and more than a little jumpy. So much for never letting her out of his sight. She watched the shallow breathing of the four dogs lying on the ground and hoped they'd make it.

She stopped in front of the first stall where she read the sign above the door. *Babe.* "Hello, Babe," she crooned. The horse's ears wiggled. She reached out a hesitant finger and stroked his long nose. From her dream, she remembered gloved hands reaching into a stall and big, scared brown eyes. Why would he steal LuAnn's horse?

"He was Michelle's favorite."

Devra spun. Mac stood close enough to touch. Her heart jumped in her chest. She stepped back against Babe's gate. Mac reached forward and took a blond curl in his grasp, letting it wrap loosely around his finger.

"I'm sorry for your loss," she said, hoping to appease the anger she could still see burning in his eyes.

He dropped the curl. His dark eyes perused her face, then moved slowly down her body. "Too bad about the dogs."

"Yeah," Devra said nervously. What was it about him that seemed so familiar?

"What do *you* think happened here?"

"I don't know," she muttered, and suddenly started to feel dizzy. The horse's wet nose slid against her neck.

She jumped forward, tripping. Mac caught her by the arms, his strong grasp holding her upright—a little too strong, a little too tight.

Babe whinnied behind her.

"What do you want?" she asked, afraid to look into those dark, rage-filled eyes.

His lips curled upward.

"What's going on?" Riley asked from the doorway.

"Just getting acquainted with your friend here." The contemptuous gleam of animosity dimmed to a cold dead hate.

Devra shivered.

"Dr. Williams is on his way," Riley said, walking into the barn.

Mac turned and left without saying another word.

"Are you all right?" Riley asked.

She nodded, though she wasn't. She wasn't anywhere near all right.

Riley reached behind her to open Babe's stall. She watched his large deft hands slip the bridle over the horse's head. "I see you've met Babe," he said and hefted a large leather saddle onto Babe's back, lifted the flaps and tightened the straps. He appeared so strong and sure of himself, so in control. "He's a gentle horse." He turned and met her eye. "He'll take good care of you."

She didn't answer, just stood staring at him. "What do you mean, take good care of me?"

"We're going for a little ride."

"Oh, no," she said, backing away from the beast. "I don't think so."

"We're going after Storm. Unless you'd rather stay here with my brother. I won't leave you by yourself."

Devra looked out the barn's opening, but didn't see a sign of Mac. "And you think I'd be safe with him?"

Riley looked at her, a strange speculative sheen in his eyes. "My brother isn't dangerous."

"Could've fooled me," she muttered.

"Stand on this," he said and gestured toward a polished stump, "then throw your leg up and over his back."

She knew this wasn't a good idea, but she wasn't about to stay there with Mac. She stepped up onto the stump as he instructed, except at the last minute Babe shifted just as she extended her leg over his saddle. "Oh!" she cried, and grabbed the saddle's horn.

With a firm grip on her shoulder and another on her rear, Riley gave her a push, righting her up on Babe's back. As she settled herself in the saddle, she could still feel the burning impression of Riley's grasp on her jeans. "Lord," she whispered. What kind of fool was she?

Riley took Babe's reins and led him around a tree. Devra clung to the horse's back, her legs holding a death grip on Babe's ribs, as she became accustomed to his height. "I don't know about this," she stammered. "I've never been on a horse before. Perhaps this isn't such a good idea." Perhaps Mac wasn't as dangerous as he appeared.

"You'll be fine," Riley assured her. He handed her the reins, then demonstrated how to get the horse to turn, first left, then right, then how to stop. "Think you can handle it?"

"Sure," she answered, though she wasn't at all sure.

"Good. I'll be right back."

She watched him hurry back to the barn, then glanced around for any sign of Mac. Something about him made her more than a little nervous. That tingling sensation tickled the back of her neck once more. Someone was out there watching her. She could feel it. She perused the bushes around her, but no one was in sight.

Not Riley.

Not Mac.

Not the man who broke into Riley's house last night. She remembered her dream vividly, could still feel the imprint of his finger on her cheek. Why couldn't she remember what he'd said to her? Thank God Riley had been there. Thank God he'd woken when he did.

Riley rode out of the barn with nothing between his jeans and the horse. "You ready?"

Her eyes widened as she took in the easy sway of man and horse. She swallowed the lump of awareness in her throat and nodded. He pointed toward a clump of trees in front of his house. Babe lurched forward as he followed Riley's horse.

As they moved, Devra could easily see the prints. First, a man's large-size boot heading toward the barn, then horses' hooves coming back out. Could he still be here?

Silently, they continued deep into the countryside. They passed under enormous crepe myrtles, their rich purple blossoms shining like amethysts in a sea of verdant green. The sweet fragrant smell teased her senses. It felt almost peaceful, like a glittery page from a children's storybook where nothing bad ever happened and people always lived happily ever after. But like so many fairy tales, nothing was ever what it seemed.

A soft, moist breeze encircled her in its embrace and lulled her into thinking the danger had passed, that everything would be all right. Then Riley stopped.

"What is it?"

"I lost his trail." Riley climbed off his horse and inspected the ground around them, which had turned pebbled like a creek bed.

"See anything?"

"No," he said after another minute had passed.

"Do you really think he's still here?"

"That depends."

"On what?"

"On what he wants."

Riley climbed back onto his horse and continued down the trail. She followed behind him, unable to shake the chill that had invaded her bones, despite the cloying heat of midday. Live oaks stretched their mammoth branches, holding thick bushels of tiny green ferns. Devra stared absently at the tiny fronds that lightly touched her cheek. A wooden structure hidden high in the branches of one such oak caught her eye. A cascade of deep fuchsia bougainvillea dropped from its wooden roof like the flowing train of a bridal veil.

Amazed, Devra stopped. Riley held a finger to his lips. Hidden beneath the thick layer of pink blossoms, Devra could see the rings of an old ladder.

"It's the perfect place to hide," he whispered. "Stay here and stay on your horse."

She nodded and watched him dismount, then silently approach the tree. He climbed the ladder and disappeared within the branches. A rustling sounded behind her. Quickly, she turned. Both horses snorted a protest, then moved with her. "Shh," she said to the animals, but didn't see anything. She moved the horses forward a few steps, her gaze searching the bushes, fear ripping down her spine. Something was here, she knew it. She *felt* it.

Perhaps in response to her apprehension, perhaps not, Babe shifted nervously and blew air loudly out of his nose. "It's okay," she cooed. But was it?

She heard a step behind her. She turned and gasped. A strong hand pressed against her mouth and before the deep chemical smell hit her, she felt herself being dragged off her horse. "No!" she screamed, but the sound came out a muffled whine. Muscle, hard as rock, pressed into her back as his vise-like grip tightened. In her last few seconds of consciousness, her one thought was of Riley.

RILEY KNEW someone had been up there the moment he entered the tree house. Nothing was out of place, but everything was just a little…different. The table and chairs by the window, the beat-up old rug on the floor, the baseball bats, gloves and balls in the wooden crate in the corner. It was all as it should be, yet somehow something was different.

Then he saw it. The folded up newspaper in the corner, an old paper, yellowed and thin. He walked closer and stared down at the picture of a young teen on the front page. "Tommy Marshall found dead at Miller's Creek" was captioned under the picture. Riley picked up the paper. The first thing he noticed was how old it was. The second was the date—almost exactly fifteen years ago.

His jaw stiffened as he stared at the paper. Someone was pulling his strings, playing him along, dropping clues for him to find: the locket, the raspberries, this fifteen-year-old paper—the *Rosemont Gazette.* Rosemont, Washington.

Washington. Wasn't that where Devra said her parents lived?

Devra. All clues always pointed back to her.

He'd left her alone too long. Someone had definitely been up here—someone who wanted him to know about the death of this boy. He tucked the paper into the waistband of his jeans and opened the hatch to climb down from the tree house, then he saw it. A chill rushed through him, making him stop and stare uncomprehendingly at the picture of his mother. It was sitting on the window's ledge.

The picture that up until now had sat on his mantel.

Riley grabbed the picture and flew down the ladder. When he got to the spot where he'd left Devra, he stood dumbfounded.

"Devra?" Where was she? "Devra!" he called, as a thin thread of panic started to wind itself tighter and tighter in his mind. His horse stood patiently waiting for him, but Devra and Babe were gone.

He tromped through the undergrowth, calling Devra's name. Had she gone back without him? Had something spooked Babe? Had their intruder found her?

The one suspect they had in Michelle's murder, the one woman who was going to be able to piece all this together for him, was gone. And he had lost her.

If anything has happened…if he were responsible for yet another woman's… He couldn't think it. How could he have left her alone? Because he hadn't believed she was in any real danger. He was so certain she had an accomplice, that she was perhaps even the killer. Certainly he hadn't expected she could end up as another victim.

The rude awakening sucker punched him in the gut. The captain was right. He wasn't thinking properly. And because of him, Devra could be dead. He had failed to protect her. He had failed—*again.*

Branches scratched his face as he tore through the thicket—calling, searching, hoping. *"Devra!"*

In the far distance, storm clouds moved across the sky. Ozone was building and he could feel the static tingling the back of his neck. He had to find her soon, before the storm drove him back.

Suddenly, he heard a soft whinny. Babe? He pushed

through a particularly nasty bramble bush, and saw Babe tied to a tree. Not just Babe, but Storm, too. Cautiously he looked around for any sign of the intruder, for any sign of Devra.

But there was none.

He checked the horses and they were fine, but where was the person who took them? Where was Devra? He started to untie the horses, when he heard something. He walked toward the sound, rounded a large tree and saw her.

His breath stuck in his throat. Mac was squatting next to her as she lay on a thick patch of grass, surrounded and practically buried in a heap of daisies. "Mac?" Riley couldn't believe his eyes. "Mac, what have you done?"

Riley didn't like the way her hands were resting on her chest, with their backs pushed together and the pinkies intertwined. He didn't like the way her hair was spread out like a fan around her head. Or the way Mac was touching it.

He stepped closer.

Mac stood, holding a daisy in his hand, confusion and pain chasing across his face.

"What happened?" Riley asked. "Is she…" He couldn't say the words, couldn't let himself absorb the emotions threatening to rack through his body.

Mac dropped the flower and it fell to Devra's side, to land atop many others. "I was looking for Storm…." He turned and looked back down at her.

Riley dropped to Devra's side and took her hand. It was still warm. She had a pulse, she was alive. Relief surged through him. He looked up at Mac.

Something dark and cold crossed Mac's face. He'd never seen Mac look like that. Almost…dangerous.

"You shouldn't have brought her here, Riley. She doesn't belong here."

Before Riley could respond, Mac disappeared through the foliage.

He rubbed Devra's hand between his own. "Devra. Come on, sweetheart. Wake up." *Please, wake up and tell me my brother had nothing to do with this.*

But he didn't like the sick sensation in his stomach, or the direction his thoughts were beginning to take. Who else would care about a picture of his mother? Who else would know the significance of that picture? Had it been Mac in his house last night?

Chapter Seven

Devra moaned as blinding pain erupted through her head. She heard her name being called and tried to open her eyes. Someone lifted her head, sending a wave of pain arcing through her skull.

"Devra, are you okay?"

It was Riley, the detective with the honey voice. She opened her eyes and tried to sit up. There were yellow daisies everywhere, on the ground, on her chest, her legs. Panic swept through her. "Get them off of me!" she cried. She swatted at them, trying to brush them away, and was overtaken by sheer hopelessness as she tried to stand, but couldn't find the strength.

"Get them off me, please," she begged.

Riley helped her to her feet and brushed the last of the blossoms away. "It's okay. They're just flowers. They can't hurt you."

She stared down at them, and even though she heard what he said, understood what he said, she was overwhelmed with the fear that they weren't just flowers, that they could hurt her.

"What happened?" he asked.

She looked up at him and tried to focus on his words, on what he wanted from her, but everything was fuzzy and it hurt to think. It hurt to move. "I'm sorry?" she asked, trying to clear the confusion from her mind.

"What is the last thing you remember?"

"Watching you climb into the tree house."

"You didn't see Mac?"

"Mac?" She shook her head. "Was he here?" Nervousness skittered along her spine.

"Mac found you."

"Oh." She looked around. "Then, where did he go?"

Riley hesitated. "What's the deal with the daisies?"

A deep shiver swept through her. Images flitted through her mind: ice-cold water, raspberries, daisies. Dizziness threatened. "I don't know," she whispered.

"What about this?" He held out a paper with a picture of Tommy on it. Tommy at thirteen. Tommy smiling and happy.

Then the shakes started and there was nothing she could do to stop them. *Tommy.* Tears filled her eyes.

He put his arms around her and pulled her close. "It's okay. Everything is going to be fine."

He said the words so easily, so casually, but nothing would be fine—not for her, not ever again.

She leaned into Riley's strong warm chest and closed her eyes, trying to forget, trying to pretend that the game wasn't up and there wasn't anywhere left for her to go or anyone out there who would help her.

Hot tears slipped out of her eyes and ran down her cheeks as the pain in her head deadened into a dull ache.

After a moment, he pulled back. "Is there anything you can tell me? What is it about this picture that has upset you?"

The paper clutched in his hand shook in the wind. She stared at it, stared at the smiling image of her childhood friend. *I'm so sorry, Tommy.*

"What is it?" Riley asked. He didn't like the look of horror that had come over her face, or the way the little color her skin had gained since waking fell away, leaving her looking like a ghostly specter as the sky darkened around them.

"They wouldn't let me say goodbye. I didn't kill him," she whispered. Her eyes filled with fear and became slightly unfocused as she stared at the paper. "You have to believe me." She sounded almost desperate and her fingers clutched his arms, clinging.

"I believe you," he whispered.

That seemed to settle her some, seemed to bring the focus back to her wild gaze as she looked up at him.

"Where did you get this?" She gestured toward the paper.

"In the tree house."

She nodded her head in quick succession. "Then he's here. He's come for me."

"Who?"

"The man who killed Tommy."

Her words chilled him. Or maybe it was the manic way in which she said them. At that moment, the wind started up, whipping through the trees, blowing her hair around her. "Who's Tommy and what does he have to do with Michelle?"

She shook her head. "I don't know."

Somewhere in the distance, thunder boomed through the sky. They had to get back to the house. "Can you ride?"

"I'll do anything to get out of here." She shivered and rubbed her arms, looking around her, her eyes searching the bushes.

He helped her up onto Babe's back. "Hang on." He grabbed Storm's reins, then climbed up on Babe behind her. "Lean back against me and hold on."

They rode as fast as they could, but had to stop for the horse he'd left tied up at the tree house, and with two horses in tow it was slow going. The storm was blowing in fast and from the look of the swollen, purple sky, it wouldn't be long before it cut loose.

The downpour started just as they rode into the barn to secure the horses. There was no sign of the dogs. "LuAnn must have them," Riley said absently.

They ran to the house. "Felix!" Devra called, and gave a look of relief as the cat came running at the sound of her voice. As Devra fed Felix, Riley called his stepmother and let her know that Storm was safe and secure in his stall in the barn.

As he hung up the phone, he turned to Devra. "We should take you to the hospital and have you examined."

She stiffened. "No."

"You don't know what happened out there. You were unconscious."

"I can't."

He shook his head in bewilderment, then picked up

the phone again to call Tony. "How's your head?" he asked as Tony's line rang.

"Better."

"Any bumps?"

"No. I wasn't hit."

"You weren't?" She hadn't mentioned that.

"No. I smelled something. Something chemical. Maybe chloroform?"

"Pretty sophisticated. Why didn't he just hit you?" She shrugged.

"Tony here," Tony said as he picked up the line.

Riley turned his attention back to the phone. "Listen, Tony. I need you out here right away. Something else has happened."

"No problem. I'm almost there."

"Almost here?"

"Yeah, the nurse at Children's worked with a police artist on a sketch of the man she saw watching Miss Morgan. The kid identified him as the guy he gave the locket to. I'd like to bring the sketch by for you and Miss Morgan to look at."

Riley raised his eyebrows. That was fast. "Good work."

"Also, I got the results back from her house. No prints on the rock."

Riley was afraid of that.

"But the prints in the house came back to a Miss Devra Miller."

Riley's grip tightened on the receiver. "Miller?"

Devra looked up at him, her eyes wide.

"Yep. Apparently, she goes by a different name."

She'd refused to be printed when they had her at the station. Now he knew why. He remembered seeing the name Miller written in the top corner of the papers describing Michelle's murder. Her deception had been right there and he'd missed it. He sat down in the chair across from her and watched as her scared gaze turned wary. Why hadn't she told him?

Riley hung up the phone and speared his hand through his hair. Uneasiness churned in his stomach. Villain or victim? Had she staged her little kidnapping? He shook his head, he just didn't know. Why would she lie about something as simple as her name? She had to know he'd find out.

"Tony's on his way."

A worried frown creased her brow. "I know."

"Are you Devra Miller?" He said the words casually, hoping for a small look of guilt or the embarrassed smile he'd seen numerous times cross her face. He waited for her to explain who she was and why she'd felt the need to go by a different name. Perhaps it was as simple as wanting a pen name for her books. She could give a little laugh and apologize, stating that she just didn't think it was important.

But she didn't say a word.

Her eyes turned cold and blank and her chameleon's mask moved into place.

"Talk to me," he demanded softly.

"There's nothing to say."

"There's a lot to say and I think you owe it to me to be honest."

"Why? Because you took me in?" Her voice was

hard, her body rigid. "I don't recall you giving me much choice."

"I want to help you."

"Why would you want to help your prime murder suspect?"

The anger emanating from her surprised him. Could he have been so wrong about her? "I know you didn't kill Michelle."

"Do you?" she mocked with arched eyebrows. "How can you be so sure?"

Exactly. Why had he been so sure?

Thunder rocked the house. Lightning forked the sky, casting an ominous glow to the room. Their silence deepened and all that could be heard was the angry beat of raindrops against the roof and bushes outside.

Devra grasped the table with splayed fingertips. "Why would Tony brave coming way out here in a torrential downpour? Just to see me? What does he really want? What aren't you telling me?"

"Don't you mean what did he find out about you? Why don't you tell me what you're hiding?"

Her dark blue eyes shimmered with frustration. Riley wanted to tell her about the sketch but, at this point, he had too many doubts about her, too many questions. Surprise would be his best strategy. He needed to study her reaction before she had time to school her features, to protect herself from whatever she might see in that sketch. It could be nothing, a nobody, a hospital orderly she'd never met. Or it could be an old lover or even an accomplice. He couldn't be sure. Not of her, not of anything.

What did Michelle's death have to do with a boy

murdered fifteen years ago? A boy Devra claimed she hadn't killed. And what did that have to do with why his mother's picture had been taken off his mantel? "If you're innocent, if you have nothing to hide, why do you care if Tony's coming over?"

"Why are you working so hard to prove I'm not innocent?"

"Dammit, Devra! Don't you think I want to believe you?"

Her eyes widened.

His tone softened. "Do you actually think I would have brought you into my home and introduced you to my family if I believed you were capable of murder?"

Tears watered her eyes and his gut clenched.

"I can't trust you," she murmured.

"You can. Open up and tell me!"

They stared at one another as the storm thundered above, the rift between them growing wider with each passing second.

"I can't help you if you won't let me in."

Headlights shone through the front windows.

"He's here," Riley said.

Devra stood, her frightened eyes growing large and filling her face.

What was she so afraid of?

Tony burst through the front door, peeled off his parka and hung it on a rack. Rainwater ran in rivulets down the slick fabric to puddle on the floor. "She's a live one. I just about drowned coming in from the car." Lightning flashed, emphasizing his words and illuminating the trees outside the window.

"Can I get you some hot tea?" Devra asked with only the slightest quiver to betray her anxiety. Riley couldn't help but be impressed by her ability to hide her emotions.

Surprise widened Tony's eyes as he stared at her. "Yes, ma'am. That'd be nice," he responded with a warm smile dimpling his cheeks.

Riley nudged him.

"Whoo-eee," Tony said as Devra left the room to get the tea. "That's quite a transformation."

"She's the same woman you saw at the station," Riley said dryly, not liking Tony ogling her.

"Nah, that woman in the station was a potted plant, this woman's a real looker."

Even though she was only wearing blue jeans and a T-shirt, the soft cotton molded Devra's curves, perfectly outlining her heart-shaped bottom and ample breasts. Her natural beauty highlighted by lustrous curls and shockingly blue eyes took Riley's breath away. Yeah, he knew how Tony felt.

"I'm not sure how she managed to hide her looks so well. That babe's a knockout. How'd I miss it?"

"She's good at hiding herself," Riley muttered. "Either that or you're one lousy cop."

"Very funny."

"I just can't stop asking myself why she's trying so hard to hide," Riley said.

"Perhaps it has something to do with our mystery man."

THE EYES of the devil.

Devra's hands trembled as she took the sketch from Tony's outstretched hand.

"Have you seen him before?"

His voice sounded as if it were traveling down a long, dark tunnel, echoing somewhere she couldn't quite place. She shifted her weight and swallowed, forcing back the rising nausea that threatened to overwhelm her. She dropped the paper on the table and fought the urge to run, to hide.

"Devra, have you seen him before?" Riley touched her arm.

She turned to him, but she didn't know what to say.

"Devra?" His tone became more determined.

She'd seen him. Every time she closed her eyes. She couldn't tear her gaze away from the picture. The artist had done an incredible job capturing the eyes. The portrayal of glimmering evil shook her to the core of her soul. "All that's missing is the sardonic twist of his lips…and the glint of laughter shining in his eyes." Everything in the room receded, so that all that was left, all she could see were coal-black graphite eyes.

"What? Devra, do you recognize him?" Tony persisted.

Devra nodded.

"Who is he?" Riley asked, stepping closer.

"The devil," she whispered, looking up at him. She reached for him as the room spun and the world tilted beneath her feet.

Strong arms caught her just before she hit the floor.

"I'm sorry," she moaned, as she pushed against Riley's arms. Suddenly, it was too hot, too stifling, too much. She had to get free. She wouldn't let them lock her up again. Not ever again. The walls moved, pushing toward her. "Please, I need air." She stood up on shaky feet and ran for the door, swinging it open.

"What happened?" Tony asked.

Riley muttered an answer she couldn't quite grasp. She stood on the porch and breathed deep gulps of air. She had to get away, just for a moment, just so she could think. She ran out into the rain, sloshing through the mud.

He was real.

They said she'd made him up. That he was a figment of her imagination, the paranoid delusions of a very sick girl.

But they were wrong.

She kept running, not sure where she was going, not caring where she was. Images flitted through her mind: cold water, daisies, raspberries, Tommy. A monster with the eyes of the devil. A monster in graphite.

Someone else had seen him, too! No longer was she the only one. Tears burned her eyes and ran down her cheeks to commingle with the rain. "You were wrong, Papa. I told you I didn't kill Tommy. I told you it wasn't me! It was him. And he's real!" She yelled the words into the night sky.

But it didn't matter. Her papa wasn't there to hear her.

Out of breath, she stopped running and bent down, bracing her hands on her knees. She looked up as the rain stopped falling—a big black hole in a sky of gray. A temporary reprieve from the downpour.

She was finally free. Someone else had seen him, too. She wasn't sick, she wasn't delusional.

"You can run, little girl."

Devra stiffened as a fierce belt of fear constricted her heart. She forced herself to take a deep painful breath. Her mind was playing tricks on her. There was no one there. She was alone.

"Mac?" she called hesitantly.

She thought again to that afternoon and the chloroform and the daisies. Why had someone gone through so much trouble to take her, then just leave her lying on the grass surrounded by daisies?

No one answered.

"Is anyone there?" She turned round and round, looking, listening. Nothing.

"But you can't hide. Not from me. Not ever."

The whispered voice stirred her memories. She'd heard those words before. She'd heard that voice before.

No! A deep guttural groan erupted from her chest. She started to run, trying to remember which way she'd come, which was the way back to Riley's house. But it was too dark. This couldn't be happening. Not again.

"Devra." The voice mocked her coming from nowhere, yet everywhere.

"Leave me alone!" she cried. God help her, she couldn't go through it again. "Riley!" she screamed. She thought she saw lights in the distance through the thick tangle of trees, and headed for them. *Please, Riley, help me.*

Laughter sounded all around her.

She pushed her legs harder, running faster, then felt a hard, bony grasp on her shoulder. She slipped, despair racking her mind. Falling…he had her.

No!

"Peekaboo, Devy. I win."

Her mind screamed, a single silent yell as she rolled through the wet mud, the leaves catching in her hair, her head hitting something hard with a searing jolt.

Not again.

Chapter Eight

When Devra woke, she was lying in her bed and two very concerned faces were staring down at her. She brought her hand up to the cut on the back of her head and winced. "What happened?"

"You fell. How are you feeling?" Riley asked.

"I don't know." She pushed herself up against the headboard. "How did I get here?"

Riley's eyes met hers. "I carried you."

Confusion tore through her. "But what about him?"

"Who?"

"The devil?" she whispered.

Riley glanced at Tony, then turned back to her. "There was no one there. You were alone."

She stared at him in disbelief. That's what everyone had said the last time. But they'd been wrong. *He* was there fifteen years ago, and he's *here* now. She wanted to plead her case, to beg them to understand, but those concerned expressions were back on their faces. They were wondering if she'd gone over the edge. They were wondering if they needed to send her to a doctor. Or perhaps even lock her up.

She wouldn't let that happen.

"I must have slipped," she said, touching her head. "Yes. The ground, it was wet. Muddy. Lots of leaves."

They nodded in agreement and relief filled their faces.

"We should call a doctor," Tony said. "She could have a concussion."

"No," she said a little too forcefully, then made herself smile. "Please. Just let me rest. It's been a long day. I'm fine. Really."

"I'll keep an eye on her," Riley said and she looked at him with gratitude.

Tony sighed. "All right. I'll come by first thing in the morning and see if you can remember anything more about our mystery man in the sketch. Okay?"

She nodded, and breathed a huge sigh of relief when both men left her room and shut the door behind them. They were getting too close. Now they knew who she was. They knew about Tommy. It wouldn't be long before they knew everything else, too. She had to leave as soon as possible. She'd find a new town, a new name, a new life. She wouldn't let them send her back to the institution.

Not ever.

"WHAT DO YOU think?" Riley asked Tony as they left the house and walked toward the barn.

"I think our Miss Morgan is coming apart at the seams."

Riley had to agree.

"What was all that talk about the devil?" Tony asked.

"I don't know. I tell you, though, nothing seems to be adding up, and she's becoming more and more unstable." They stopped outside the barn's entrance and

Riley turned back to glance at Devra's window. He speculated what she was planning and how much longer it would be before she disappeared. He'd have to keep a real close eye on her.

"I'll agree with that," Tony said, following his gaze.

Riley turned and opened the door, then entered the barn. They approached the horse stalls and made sure all the horses were fed and bedded down for the night.

"If there's any possibility she's our killer—" Tony started.

Riley knew what he was going to say. He didn't want to admit that perhaps he'd been wrong. Maybe bringing Devra to his home had been a terrible mistake. "Let's look at the facts," he started. "We've had four women killed."

"All dead ringers for Devra," Tony added.

"All women who were murdered in the same city as she was then living."

"But why leave her jewelry at the crime scene?" Tony asked. "That just doesn't make sense."

"Maybe she's left tokens at all the crime scenes and this was the first time they've been able to trace one back to her. Make sure to check out that angle." But even as Riley said the words, they didn't sound like Devra. He couldn't imagine her killing, let alone methodically placing clues on the victim, hoping the police would find her. *Would stop her?*

"All right, but what about our mystery man? Our devil in the sketch," Tony asked.

Riley nodded. "There has to be someone. Both the nurse and the boy couldn't be wrong."

"An accomplice?" Tony asked.

"Or a stalker."

"Then why not take her out when he had the chance this afternoon?"

Riley shook his head. "I don't know, and I don't understand what any of this has to do with me and my family."

"You mean the picture of your mom in the tree house?"

"Exactly."

"Maybe this doesn't have anything to do with the victims looking like Devra. Maybe it has always been about them looking like Michelle."

As Riley absorbed Tony's words, trepidation crawled over his skin. "If that's true then bringing Devra here could have put her in even greater danger."

Tony walked out the barn's doorway. "It's something to think about. Why else would anyone care about a picture of your mom, unless they were trying to get to you?"

What else could someone do to try to get to him? They'd already killed Michelle; would Devra be next? Riley watched Tony get in his car and drive away. He replayed their conversation again and again in his mind as he locked up the barn. There was only one direction that line of thinking could follow—Mac. But Mac had always loved Michelle. Hadn't he?

THE ESTATE lay in a thick shroud of darkness, the only light coming from the quarter moon as the clouds raced across its surface. He walked quickly, his boots making soft mucking noises as he crossed the wet earth beneath the thick canopy of trees. He followed the path along the river, moving closer to the house, moving closer to Devra.

His footsteps crushed the fragile azalea petals the storm had shaken loose from their branches. As the path curved around the house, the barn came into view. He stopped and listened to the whimpering of restless animals. Bright lights shone down on the cop as he locked up the barn for the night, protecting it from any further intrusions.

He laughed under his breath and unsheathed a serrated knife from its leather case. He crept closer, smiled and raised the blade. "This one's for you, Devra."

DEVRA'S SLEEP was far from peaceful. She moaned, tossing and turning. She felt like she couldn't breathe, as if a heavy weight were pushing down on her chest. Pulling herself from the dream, she opened her eyes and gasped as Felix's yellow gaze gleamed in the dim light from his perch on her chest. The last remnants of her dream snapped into place.

"Riley!" Oh, no! She pushed the cat off her, jumped out of bed and ran to the window. Riley was outside and walking toward the house.

But he wasn't alone.

Horror clogged her throat. She fumbled with the guillotine window but couldn't get it open. The man behind him lifted a knife. She banged her fists against the glass and screamed, "Riley! Behind you!"

Riley turned. The man lunged. They fell, rolling

her knees buckled and she dropped into the mud. She hadn't been able to shoot. Once the intruder had picked up his knife, he could have easily killed Riley. She hadn't been strong enough to do what it took to protect him, to protect herself.

He had to be the man from the sketch…the man from her *dreams*. She should have told Riley about him earlier. If she'd told him that he'd chased her through the woods, maybe he would have been more careful. She had been so afraid he wouldn't believe her. And because of that fear, he almost died.

Suddenly, she knew the devil was right—she could run, but she couldn't hide. A sudden onslaught of bone-deep chills overtook her. She couldn't stop him. It was as if she were thirteen years old all over again and she was alone and helpless, misunderstood and without hope.

The tremors cascading through her grew with each passing second, with each passing thought. He would kill Riley, just like he had Tommy, because of her. Because death was her constant companion and anyone who came near her, anyone who cared about her, died.

She hadn't seen Riley approach, but suddenly he was kneeling before her, prying the gun out of her hands. "It's okay," he said. "He's gone. Are you all right?"

She stared at him and tried to make sense of his words. All right? She didn't think she'd ever be all right. Not again.

The rain had matted down his hair and washed most of the mud from his face. He looked okay, except for a few scratches and an ugly red swelling on the side of his face. She wanted to wipe the blood off his cheek, but couldn't quite bring herself to touch him.

"Thanks for the save." He placed his hand over hers, hanging midair between them, and brought it to his cheek.

He was warm. He was alive. His touch was gentle, too gentle. Suddenly, something broke within her and she was flooded with emotion. Tears streamed down her face. "I was so scared. I couldn't move. I couldn't shoot him."

"Shh," he murmured. "It's okay."

"I'm so sorry. I did this. I brought death to your door."

"I'm not dead. See, I'm right here." His lips lifted in a small smile. "You're not responsible."

She shook her head. "He's found me again. He always does. I have to go. I have to get out of here. Running, that's all I can do." Her shaking became violent.

He wrapped his arms around her and pulled her close to him, rubbing his hands up and down her back. "You don't have to go. We can fight him together. You're not in this alone."

Alone. His words reverberated in her mind. Of course she was alone. She had always been alone. She clung to his chest. His warmth seeped into her skin, melting the ice in her veins, dulling the sharp edge of fear that was slicing through her ability to think.

He was so strong, yet gentle at the same time. She clutched his rock-hard arms as a fine sprinkling of rain fell upon them, cleansing them of the mud and the horror. She took a deep breath as her heartbeat slowed and tender warmth filled her. He smelled so good—rich, earthy, the scent of man. A man who could protect her. A man who could love her?

She was afraid to look up, afraid to meet his eyes. Afraid if she did, she'd see that she was fooling herself. That he didn't care about her, wouldn't be there for her, didn't believe in her. Then she'd have to let him go.

And be alone.

And cold.

And scared.

Again.

"You should have run," he said. "You shouldn't have taken the chance. What if something had happened to you?"

"I couldn't let him hurt you." Her voice trembled as she said the words.

"Why not?" He lifted her chin, his gaze probing hers.

A shudder whispered through her. "Every other time the dreams…they came too late to help. Watching people die—" She shook her head. "It doesn't matter what could have happened to me, what matters is that nothing happened—"

He tilted his head, bringing his face closer.

Her gaze dropped to his lips. She tried to fight it, tried to force herself to look away.

"—to you," she whispered.

His head dropped lower, his lips mere inches from hers.

She swayed, her hands on his chest moving ever so slightly upward. His mouth barely touched hers—soft, sweet, gentle. He moved his lips over hers, parting them, softly nibbling. Languid warmth, like thick, hot honey, spread through her, weakening her legs.

His tongue slipped into her mouth. She graciously welcomed it, savoring his taste. Seductive heat melted her limbs. She moaned and wrapped her arms around his neck, pulling herself closer to him, reveling in the way his hard, strong chest felt against her. It had been so long since she'd felt this way. She didn't want it to stop.

"You taste good, sugar," he mumbled as he broke for air.

His words quickened her blood. Light-headed, she lingered, her lips trailing the corner of his mouth. "I don't know if it's right, but I need you."

"It's right," he breathed, and moved his lips down the side of her neck, teasing the sensitive skin at the base of her throat. A soft moan escaped her as the warmth flowing through her body heated, moving faster, and bringing with it a tension that ached to be sated.

Sated by him.

"Please," she moaned. She was finding it hard to breathe.

"Please what?" he asked.

The husky rasp of his voice, the quickening of his touch led her to believe that her effect on him might be as strong as his on her. The thought was intoxicating. "Please don't let me go. I don't want to be alone. Not tonight."

Riley picked her up and carried her into the house, then set her down and locked the door behind him. She was looking up at him with those incredible blue eyes and it was all he could do not to pull her wet nightshirt over her head and make love to her right there on the floor.

"Make love to me, Riley. Make me forget. Just for tonight." The small embarrassed smile he'd come to love was back.

Her words lit a fire within him, and he felt himself thicken with need. *Mon Dieu*, Riley had never wanted anything in his life as much as he wanted this woman at this moment. But he couldn't have her. He knew he couldn't. It was unethical, it was wrong. She was vulnerable.

She was beautiful.

He kissed her gently, softly, his own need dangerously close to the perilous point. He had to focus on why she was there and on the case that seemed to be growing more dangerous and explosive by the moment. "Darlin', I'd love to take you into my room and love you all night, but I don't think that would be best for either of us right now."

A flicker of pain leapt from her eyes.

He pulled her to him. "I'm sorry," he whispered.

She stiffened, but he held tight.

"Soon," he promised. "As soon as we find our way clear of this case. Because, honey, I want you. Real bad."

She relaxed and pulled back. "You mean as soon as you decide I'm not a killer."

He shook his head, but she stepped away from him, walking past him to her room.

"Damn," he muttered, but she was right. He had to make sure she wasn't guilty, but even more he had to make sure she was sane.

Chapter Nine

The next morning, Riley woke to a loud pounding on his front door. He swore as he stared at the clock: 6:00 a.m. Who could be here this early? "Hold your horses!" he yelled as the pounding persisted. He climbed out of bed, pulled on a pair of jeans, then walked bare-chested to the front door.

He swung it open and was surprised to find his father standing before him, red-faced and steaming. "Dad, what is it?" he asked, instantly concerned. He couldn't remember the last time he'd seen his dad so worked up, or the last time he'd come to his doorstep.

"You got a minute?" his dad asked, his expression hard, his voice cold as he walked into the room.

Riley stepped back. "Sure. Give me a second and I'll grab a shirt."

"Don't bother."

Riley paused at the acid tone in his voice. "All right. What's up?"

"I want to know how you can have so little regard for your job and your family that you would bring *that* woman here." His father raised a trembling hand and pointed it at him. "I saw you last night all over the woman who could very well have killed your brother's wife."

Riley stood dumbstruck. His father had been there last night, watching them? He couldn't help feeling like a child as the sting of his father's venom swept through him. He took a deep breath. "*Could* is the operative word, Dad. She's innocent."

"Think with your head, Riley."

"Why can't you give me the benefit of the doubt? Trust, for once in your life, that maybe I know what I'm doing."

"I wish I could, but you always seem to step over the line, to push the envelope and damn the consequences."

Riley cringed at his words, but knew there wasn't anything he could say or do to change his father's opinion of him. There never had been. He held his father's heated gaze and refused to back down. "I think with my head, but mostly I think with my gut. That's who I am. Take it or leave it."

His father stiffened. "You've always been like that. Why couldn't you have learned to stay within your boundaries? When will you ever accept the consequences of your actions?"

"Why don't you come right out and say it? You think it's my fault, don't you?"

"You couldn't control what Michelle did."

"I'm not talking about Michelle. I'm talking about Mom and we both know it."

His father opened his mouth to respond but, at that

moment, Tony stepped through the open doorway, a grim look on his face and a manila folder in his hand.

"Sorry to interrupt. You got any coffee on?" His eyes were bloodshot, his clothes rumpled and he looked in desperate need of a sharp razor.

Riley took a deep breath and glanced from Tony to his dad, then back to Tony. "No, but we can fix some." He turned toward the kitchen.

Unfortunately, his father followed.

"What happened to your face?" Tony asked.

"We had an intruder last night right after you left. He attacked me outside as I was coming back from the barn." He looked at his dad. "Devra came out with my gun and scared him off."

Tony's eyes widened in astonishment. "Did you get a good look at him? Was he our devil?"

"I don't know. We were pretty muddy." He turned to his father. "What about you, Dad? Did you see anything?"

His father shook his head. "I'll leave you two to your business. Riley, I hope you'll keep in mind what I said."

"Don't see how I couldn't." As he watched his father walk out of the room, he wondered if he'd ever be able to please him. Then he wondered why he still bothered trying. He turned and filled the coffee machine with water and coffee.

"What did I walk in on?" Tony asked, leaning against the wall. "It seemed pretty intense."

Riley shook his head. "Old family stuff."

Tony nodded and let it go. "The captain wants to talk with you about your conversation with Nurse Jenkins."

"Yeah?"

"He also found out Devra was staying here."

Riley swore. Now he knew where his father had gotten his information.

"You might as well bring Devra in with you," Tony continued. "I'm sure he'll want to speak with her, too, once I tell him what I've discovered."

Riley's stomach dropped.

Tony continued, "The last time Devra used the name Miller she lived in Seattle. I contacted an old college buddy of mine who lives up there and had him do some checking into her background."

Riley forced himself to appear neutral. Devra had risked her life for him. She had gone up against their intruder, against the man who more than likely had killed Michelle. She was as much a victim in this mess as the rest of them. So why the secrets?

"What'd your buddy find?" he asked, even though a part of him didn't want to know. With a lurch, he realized that he'd broken his number one rule—he'd let himself become emotionally involved with a suspect.

Not a suspect, a victim, he reminded himself.

He pulled two cups from the cupboard as Tony slid a fax of an old police file across the table. Riley looked down into the scared eyes of a young girl—a young Devra.

"She'd been arrested when she was thirteen for the murder of a neighbor boy," Tony explained. "No one ever discovered exactly what had happened that day, but the kid had his head smashed in and his blood was all over her. They found her wandering the forest in a daze, a rock covered with the kid's blood in her hand."

Riley set down the cups and dropped into a chair to scan the file. "Tommy Marshall," he muttered, and cursed aloud. He remembered the way she'd looked when he'd shown her the newspaper article of Tommy's death, the way she'd clutched him. He looked up at Tony. "She said she didn't kill him."

Tony's lips thinned into a straight line.

Riley turned back to the papers. "How did your friend get his hands on a juvenile's sealed file?"

"Apparently, the police chief was the victim's father. He believes she did it, and he's still carrying a grudge."

Riley nodded. "It says here they released her."

"Yep, not enough evidence. Burns the chief up, though. It's a good thing she lives far away from Washington."

Riley dropped the fax onto the table next to the sketch of their "devil" and rose to pour them both a cup of much-needed coffee. "There you go," he said without turning. "She wasn't convicted. I don't see any reason to drag this whole sordid mess out now, especially since none of this information is admissible."

"There you go, nothing," Tony sputtered, as outrage crossed his face. "Aren't you the one who says where there's smoke—"

Riley handed Tony a cup. "Yeah, look for the fire."

"Well, this broad's smoking more than my uncle Sal's old diesel pickup truck."

Riley's smile was grim. He walked over to the counter and picked up the paper he'd found in the tree house. "When Devra saw this, she freaked. She swears the man who killed Tommy is here and with all the stuff that's been happening around here, I'm starting to believe her."

Tony looked at the paper with quiet speculation.

"I'll wake Devra," Riley offered. "I'm sure she can explain what happened."

"Good. 'Cause I, for one, sure would like to hear about it and the sooner, the better."

"She swears she didn't do it."

"And you believe her?"

Riley nodded. He did. He just hoped he was right, for all their sakes.

Tony sighed, and the tension dropped from his shoulders. "I'm so tired I can hardly see straight, let alone think."

Riley grinned, hoping to lighten the air between them. "Oh, is that what's wrong with you? I thought you were just getting downright ugly in your old age."

"Hardy har har."

"And you could use a shower, too, man. Whoo-eee."

"You're just a barrel of laughs," Tony muttered as Riley walked toward Devra's room.

Riley knocked softly on the door and wondered how she would greet him, if it'd be with open arms or embarrassment. He hoped she didn't think their kiss had been a mistake. Walking away from her had been one of the hardest moves he'd ever made, but he was glad he hadn't given in to his growing attraction to her in light of what they'd have to discuss this morning. He had to be on guard, to keep himself at a distance; otherwise, he'd never be able to allow Tony and the captain to question her. She had risked her life for him, he would never forget that.

He knocked softly. After a moment, he knocked again, then turned the door handle and walked in. "Hey, sleepyhead," he called softly, but the words died on his lips. Devra wasn't in the room. Her bed was made and a note lay on her pillow. He picked up the note.

Dear Riley,
"Thank you for your hospitality," doesn't seem enough after all we've shared. As you might have guessed, the man who took my locket, the man in the sketch, is the same man who killed Michelle. I am certain of this, because when I was a child, I saw this man kill a friend of mine and he's haunted me ever since. I must go before I put you and your family in further danger. I can't bear to witness the death of another person I care about. I'll treasure the time we spent together. My only wish is that we had more.
Fondly,
Devra.
P.S. You'll find your car at my house.

Riley winced. If she was so certain this man from her past was Michelle's killer, why didn't she stay? Why didn't she confide in him? Why didn't she trust him? He walked back into the kitchen.

Tony took one look at his face and said, "She's gone?"

Riley nodded and dropped the note onto the table.

Tony shook his head. "How far can a lady and her cat get? We're in the boondocks out here."

"She took my car. She's scared and she's running from whomever she saw in this sketch, from whoever attacked me last night." He pointed to the drawing on the table, but even as the excuse tumbled off his tongue, he tensed with frustration. He could have taken care of her; he could have taken care of them both.

Tony took another slug off his cup. "Guess I can forget about that nap."

"Guess so," Riley agreed and left the room to finish getting dressed.

Five minutes later, they climbed into Tony's car. "She couldn't have had too much of a head start on us," he reasoned, but couldn't help but feel relieved when he saw his Expedition parked on the street, and Devra's Suburban still in the driveway outside her house.

"Listen, Tony. Do me a favor and drop me off. I need time to convince her that she should be the one to tell the captain about Tommy. It's the best way to defuse the situation."

Tony threw him a skeptical look. "Are you sure you're being objective here about our pretty Miss Morgan?"

Riley sighed. "I'm trying. If she doesn't talk to him then I'll go in and do it myself. Trust me, Tony. I'm following my gut here, and my gut says she's innocent."

"What about our talk last night about her coming unhinged?"

"That was before she went after the intruder with my gun. Besides, last night Mac looked just as good a suspect as she did. I think there's a lot more to this puzzle that we need to figure out and my money is still on Devra giving us the pieces."

"All right," Tony relented. "You're lucky I was up half the night and am exhausted. I'll give you a call around four." He pulled over and let Riley out.

"Thanks," Riley said as he hopped out of the car. He watched Tony drive away, then hurried up the walk just as Devra came out the front door with boxes teetering in her arms.

"Riley," she gasped.

"Morning, doll."

Without looking him in the eye, she handed him a box. "I'm glad you're here," she said with a little laugh that didn't quite ring true. "I absolutely hate being here alone."

"Then why chance coming back? Why not ask for help?"

She grimaced and, for a second, had the decency to look sorry for running out on him.

"Where are you going?" he asked.

"Far away from here," she responded with dead seriousness.

Did she really not trust him to help her? To protect her? He cringed as the words ran through his mind. He was lousy at protection. He hadn't been able to stop his mother from being killed right in front of him, nor had he been able to help Michelle. He pushed down the utter feeling of failure that swept through him every time he thought of it and focused on Devra. "Stay and let me help you. We can figure this out."

She stopped, dropped the boxes in the back of her Suburban and stared at him. "Didn't you get my note?"

He didn't respond.

"Well, then, you know I can't." She grabbed the boxes he'd been holding and slid them in the back hatch with the others.

He leaned against the car. "You're leaving to protect me?"

"That's right. And the rest of your family. That man could have killed you last night."

Did she really think he couldn't take care of himself? Stunned, Riley stared at her. "Or you," he countered.

She stopped, but still didn't look at him. "Exactly."

"In other words, you don't trust me to do my job to keep you or myself safe?"

Devra took a deep breath and turned to him. She could hear the hurt pride in his tone, could see it in his eyes. She softened. Suddenly, the fear she'd been keeping at bay, refusing to think about, swarmed inside her.

"Do you think it's a coincidence that you and Michelle are both blue-eyed, curly-haired blondes?" he asked.

"No," she whispered.

"And that you both fit the profile of other victims. Victims, I might add, who were found in cities where you lived. Didn't you think it was just a matter of time before he came after you?"

She stared into his eyes, willing him to understand. "He did last night and you almost paid the price." She reached for him, and ran the tip of her finger along the bruises on the side of his face. He caught her hand in his, the contact sending a deep ache straight to her heart. "I have to leave. I have to go somewhere where he won't be able to find me." But even as she said the words, she knew it wasn't possible. She knew wherever she'd gone he'd always been able to find her.

You can run, little girl, but you can't hide.

"He's found you before."

His words echoed her thoughts, sending a feeling of fatalism bearing down on her. It was true. There was nothing she could do. Nowhere she could go. *But at least he won't hurt you, too.*

"Let me help you." His dark brown eyes pleaded with her.

"What do you suggest?"

"That you're the one who needs protecting. Don't leave. Trust me."

She wished she could.

"Stay."

As his eyes met hers, she turned away, afraid she was folding, afraid she'd give in. If she did, then what? Then her nightmares would finally catch up with the both of them. "I thought you weren't in the protection business," she countered.

"I'm not." He grabbed her, refusing to let her turn away from him, and pulled her roughly against him, his strong arms banding around her as if he'd never let her go. "But for you, I will be."

The warmth of his embrace, the utter feeling of safety almost undid her. "Why would you do that for me? I was running out on you. You never would have heard from me again."

Regret flashed through his eyes, then disappeared so quickly she wasn't sure it had ever been there. "Good question. I guess I'm not ready for you to run off and leave me yet."

Was it possible? Could she really trust him?

"But I need something from you first."

Her balloon of hope filled with lead and dropped to the pit of her stomach. "What?"

"I need you to come into the house, fix me a cup of coffee and tell me exactly what's been going on. Especially about Tommy Marshall. Everything. Got it?"

She looked into his face and wondered if she could tell him everything. Could she trust him that much?

Chapter Ten

As Devra stared at Riley, she knew she couldn't take the chance. She couldn't tell him everything, but she could tell him about Tommy. She just wasn't sure if she was ready to unearth and relive all the memories.

He led her into the kitchen, where she poured them both cups of coffee, then sat next to him at the table.

"It's really okay," he said encouraging her. "I'm not here to judge."

"What do you want to know?"

"Let's start at the beginning. Let's start with Tommy Marshall."

She nodded; it was inevitable that he'd find out. She couldn't hide from what happened, but still she was reluctant to let her mind go back to that day fifteen years ago. "As far back as I can remember I'd had a normal life. Some would even say an ideal life. I grew up in a small town in Washington State." She took a long sip from her cup. "Every free moment I had I played in the forest."

He nodded, encouraging her to continue.

"That particular day was one of those rare sunshine-filled days when the big leaf maples with their thick undergrowth of ferns and ivy came to life in a sea of green." The memories started filtering back. "Tommy was my best friend and closest neighbor." A small smile touched her lips. "He had stepped out of the bushes, joining me on a rock beside the river with a large bowl of wild raspberries in his hand."

She remembered he'd handed her the bowl and she'd taken a bite of the soft fruit, all the while wondering if he'd noticed her chest had begun to develop. She closed her eyes as the memories of that long-ago day washed over her and suddenly she was thirteen years old again, and Tommy was the light of her life.

Wanna go for a swim? he asked, a wicked grin splitting his face.

You crazy? That water's freezing.

I'll keep you warm.

He waggled his eyebrows and she imagined him holding her tight, the way they do in the movies, causing a rush of embarrassment to streak across her cheeks.

Don't be silly, Tommy Marshall, she said and, laughing, threw a handful of river pebbles at him.

Come on, Devra. You're thirteen years old now. Don't you think it's time you stop acting like a kid? He reached out and touched the daisy she had tucked behind her ear.

A strange rush of excitement quickened her blood, making her almost dizzy. *W-what do you mean?* she stammered. How was she still acting like a kid?

We could…um. I mean, how about if we kissed?

Shock washed over her and her heart started to pound. Tommy had never talked to her that way before. Though, she had to admit she liked it, just a little. She did want to kiss him, had even dreamed about kissing him. He must have read the look on her face, for he pushed the raspberry bowl nestled between them to the side and leaned forward, his lips inches from hers.

She stared into the green depths of his eyes, afraid to move.

Close your eyes, he whispered.

Obediently, she did, as anticipation rushed through her. His soft lips falling tenderly across her own sent her soaring.

A twig broke.

The blood rushed to her head, making it swim.

A shadow fell across her face.

Laughter bubbled inside her. She was so deliriously happy.

A sharp thud.

Tommy fell to the side, his shoulder knocking into her.

Devra opened her eyes.

"I can't," she said to Riley. "I can't go back there." Her heart was pounding so hard she could barely breathe.

"You can. He can't hurt you. I'm here." He hesitated a moment, then pulled her onto his lap and wrapped her in his arms. "I'm right here. Tell me what happened."

Her first instinct was to pull away. But he was so warm and comforting, and she felt safe in his arms, safer than she ever remembered feeling. She took a deep

breath, and continued. "Tommy and I were…talking by
the river. He gave me my first kiss. My eyes were
closed, and the next thing I knew he was lying on the
rocks in the shallow water. Blood was oozing from the
side of his head and running down his cheek."

She shuddered as the images barraged her. "His
wide, unblinking eyes were staring at me. I screamed
and tried to back away from him, but I couldn't move.
My hand had landed in the bowl of raspberries, squish-
ing the berries. I tried to wipe them off on my blouse,
but there was blood all over me. Tommy's blood." She
swiped at the tear running down her cheek and nestled
deeper into Riley's lap.

He held her and murmured in her ear. "It's okay."

But it wasn't okay, it would never be okay. She knew
that now. "Stones crunched behind me. I scrambled to
my feet and there he was, watching me."

"The man in the sketch?"

She nodded. "The look of the devil Papa had always
preached about glowing in his eyes. A large rock covered with blood was clutched in his hand and his lips
were curved in a triumphant smile." She stiffened. "Oh,
God!"

"What?" He clutched her tighter.

"I remember what he said to me." She couldn't
breathe, couldn't think, just kept hearing his voice whispering in her mind.

"Peekaboo."

Suddenly, she was a child again and, like the prover-
bial spilt milk, the images wouldn't stop flowing. She'd
turned and ran up the bank of the river and into the

northwestern woods she knew like the back of her hand. "No matter how fast I ran, every time I'd turn he was still behind me. After a while, I was so tired. I stopped to lean against a tree and slid down its trunk."

She took a deep breath. "Then I saw him. He was still holding the bloody rock in his hand, still smiling. He wasn't even breathing hard. I remember being so scared, I remember freezing as his eyes met mine. 'You can run, little girl, but you can't hide. Not from me.' Those are the words he said to me. The words I keep hearing again and again."

Just like last night.

She clenched her fists and forced herself to continue, when all she really wanted to do was get into her car and drive far, far away. "I ran in so many directions, I was no longer sure where I was, or which way was which. I remember the river looming ahead of me. I remember thinking if I could just reach the river's path, I could follow it back home. Back to Papa. But I slipped on a patch of wet pine needles. The pain in my left ankle almost brought me down, but I knew I couldn't fall. I knew if I did, I wouldn't be able to get back up. So I kept running, no longer caring about the path or the pain."

She hesitated.

"Go on," he encouraged. "You're doing fine."

"As I reached the river, a large hand grasped my shoulder and pulled me backward. I fell to the ground. The impact knocked the air from my chest. Pain sliced through my head. Something wet and sticky ran down the side of my face."

She touched her cheek. "I begged him not to hurt me.

He leaned over me, his face coming closer. Then blackness swallowed the light. The last image I saw before succumbing to the darkness was a glint of red laughter shining through obsidian eyes."

The eyes of the devil.

"Those are the eyes I saw depicted in the sketch of Michelle's killer. It's him. He killed Tommy."

Riley stared at her, unblinking.

"I know it sounds crazy. It is crazy. This whole situation is crazy. What's worse is that's all I can remember of that day. They said they found me in the forest with the murder weapon in my hand. But I can't remember what happened. I don't know why he let me go. I don't know why he didn't kill me, too." She let out a deep breath, trying to fight back the tears that were threatening to overwhelm her.

"Why have you kept running? Why haven't you let somebody help you?"

"Who? The police? I can't take that risk again."

"What risk?"

"That they'd lock me up." She clung to shoulders that felt strong enough to hold up the world, but were they strong enough for her and for what the future may hold? "I can't go through that again," she insisted. "I can't have everyone calling me a killer."

"They won't."

"Tommy's parents believed I killed him, and so did mine. The police just wanted the case solved. They took the easy way. They didn't care whose life they were ruining or whose dreams they destroyed. Chief Marshall was so certain it was me."

Riley cringed at her words.

"Please, Riley. Don't make me go through that again. Let me leave. I'll be more careful. I won't let him find me."

Her eyes pleaded with him and as much as he wanted to help her, he couldn't stand the idea of her out there on her own with a madman on her heels. "I can't. I'm sorry." Tears spilling onto her cheeks broke his heart. "You can't keep running and hiding," he said. "You deserve more, you deserve a life."

"I can't stay. He almost killed you last night. He'll be back again."

"Bah," he scoffed. "He didn't even come close." He pulled her close and breathed deep her vanilla scent. "I want you to stay."

Her eyes locked on his. "You're what I'll miss most about New Orleans."

"If you want me as much as I want you, if you want your freedom, then take it. Don't let anyone or anything stop you. Not even your fear."

"But how? What can I do?"

"Fight back."

She shook her head. "I've never been a fighter. I wouldn't know where to begin. I'm not that strong."

Riley stared at her. Was that really what she thought? "Don't kid yourself, Devra. How many people could have dealt with what you've been running from all these years?"

She didn't answer him, just ran her fingers across his collarbone, studying it as if it held the answers to all life's secrets.

"Not many," he continued. "They would have ended up in the loony bin blabbering to the padded walls."

She dropped her head as another tear escaped out the corner of her eye. "Maybe that's where I belong," she said softly, so softly he almost didn't hear her.

"Maybe," he challenged.

She looked up at him, afraid and confused.

"There's only one way to find out."

"How's that?" she asked warily.

"Go back to where it all started and do the research the cops never did. You're a grown woman now, not some kid to be discounted. Find out what really happened to Tommy. Stop running and fight for the truth."

Her eyes widened at his words. "I couldn't."

"Why not?"

"I'm afraid," she admitted.

"Of what? The killer? Or that you may find out everyone was right, that you killed Tommy."

Misery chased across her face and he knew his words had hit a sore spot. He knew what he'd just verbalized was exactly what she'd been afraid of all these years. He took her hands into his own and gave them a squeeze. "These hands are connected to a heart, which beats in time to a special soul. Your soul. I know you're not capable of that kind of evil. You didn't kill Tommy, Michelle or anyone else. I believe that with everything I am."

Tears were flowing again, filling big blue eyes full of gratitude. "Please come with me," she said softly. "I can't face them alone."

"Your fears?"

"My parents."

"Oh." He nodded understanding, knowing exactly how it felt to face a parent whose disappointment shone through his eyes like beacons in the night. "You're stronger than you give yourself credit for."

She shook her head. "I'm not. I can't do it on my own. I need you."

No one had ever said those words to him before. The warmth they inspired was totally unexpected. She wrapped her arms around his neck. Her warmth, her softness, her sweet breath on his neck as she clung to him had him considering her request. It would be disastrous for his career and he could lose his job, his reputation. And he knew that what little respect his father had left for him would be gone if they didn't find the answers they were searching for. But his father would also not forgive him if he let Michelle's killer go free. Devra—and her past—held the key to that killer. And that past was in Washington.

He'd given Tony his word he'd go to the station. With Devra. "My captain wants to ask me a few questions. Tony found out about Tommy. You should come in and tell the captain the truth. It will sound better coming from you. Trust me."

She sat back, her eyes widening. "The charges were dropped. There wasn't enough evidence against me. How did he get his hands on juvenile records?"

"Chief Marshall's still carrying a grudge. A big one."

She stared at him for a minute. "Riley, I can't go anywhere near the station. I just can't. If I do, they won't let me leave. I won't be able to go back and discover the truth." She grabbed his arm.

"I don't have a choice, Devra."

She let go of his arm and walked over to the window. After a moment, she turned back to him. "I know. I guess we'll just have to take our chances with your captain."

But Riley knew she had a point. Once she went into the station and told her story, everything would change. If the captain believed her, especially after the incident last night, then she would be put in protective custody. If the captain didn't believe her, then she would be watched day and night. Either way, Riley was certain he wouldn't be the one allowed near her. "All right," he relented. "I'll go in and see the captain alone."

She blew out a sigh of relief, then smiled. "I knew I could trust you."

"Really?" he asked amused. "When did you come to that realization?"

"Just now."

He pulled her into his arms. "You better." His lips brushed tenderly across hers, sparking something within him. He held her closer, his mouth moving hungrily over hers. She responded by clinging to him as if this were the last time they'd be together. A twinge of panic tightened his gut. "You'll be here when I get back?" He pulled back so he could read the truth in her eyes.

She touched her swollen lips, tempting him to pull her into his arms once more, and stared up at him with melting blue eyes. "Yes, I'll be here," she said softly.

And he believed her. He didn't know why, but they seemed to have crossed some line and he believed that she wouldn't lie to him, that she'd trust him to help her. He relaxed and gave her a gentle smile. "Good, pack only what you need. No reason to let anyone think you fled town. We'll take my car."

She nodded. He left to face the captain, hoping it wouldn't be for the last time. An hour later, he returned from the station. The captain had been tough, but Riley held his ground and got through their meeting with his job intact, and without bringing up Tommy Marshall. Hopefully, he'd even managed to buy them the few days they needed to uncover whatever secrets were buried in the small town of Rosemont, Washington, before anyone back at the station discovered he'd absconded with their number one suspect.

With Felix tucked in his carry cage and a couple overnight bags stowed in the back, they piled into Riley's Expedition and drove out of the Garden District. Devra leaned her head against the window and sighed. "I hope I make it back here someday."

"You will," Riley assured her. But as New Orleans fell farther and farther behind them, he couldn't help wondering if he'd made the right decision. Was he following his gut, or was something else driving him? He wasn't sure, but somewhere along the way he'd begun to care about this lost woman. Worse, he felt a need to protect her. As the sun caught a golden curl, enticing him to touch it, he turned away and hoped he wasn't making the biggest mistake of his life.

Chapter Eleven

They drove all day and most of the night, each taking turns while the other napped. Around three in the morning, Devra pulled into a rest stop and slept because her vision had become too blurry to continue driving safely. Three hours later, Riley woke and started them on their journey again. By the end of the second day, they couldn't take the long hours in the car and pulled into a motel parking lot for a much needed night of sleep. As soon as her head hit the pillow, Devra was out.

SHE WAS RUNNING again. Dwarfed by the large trees, she ran, pushing her way through the green leaves, wincing as the branches whipped across her face. Somewhere in the darkness behind her, she could hear his breathing echoing through the trees. Footsteps thumped against the forest floor.

Riley, help me! She turned, looking behind her, searching for the handsome face with the dark brown, smiling eyes. But he wasn't there. The river loomed ahead of her. Panic squeezed her throat shut and she couldn't make a sound, couldn't call for help, couldn't scream. She pushed harder, afraid to look back. Bony fingertips reached, grasping, pulling.

Riley!

SHE WOKE CHOKING, her eyes flying open, his name still on her lips. She felt the bed move and suddenly he was next to her, staring down at her with those dark brown eyes, and she could hardly breathe.

"Devra? What is it?" Riley asked.

The warm timbre of his voice reached out to stroke her tattered nerves. As she stared at him, the air whooshed into her lungs. She tried to shake herself loose of fear's grip, but the weight of impending doom lingered. "Nothing. Just another dream."

"Not of our…" He didn't complete the sentence, but she knew who he meant.

"No, just a plain old everyday normal nightmare," she lied, not wanting to discuss it.

He smiled and brushed the hair back from her face. She pushed the last vestiges of her dream away and tried not to think about how they were changing, and how they seemed to come more often. She closed her eyes and let his soft touch soothe away the darkness and wrap her in languid warmth.

"Riley," she whispered. She opened her eyes and her gaze met his. Something shifted in his eyes, his breathing quickened and suddenly she was aware of strong arms next to her. Her breathing went shallow and she couldn't help staring at his lips, couldn't help wondering if he'd kiss her again.

He leaned closer, lying on the bed next to her. "I won't let anything happen to you."

"Promise?" she asked, but the word caught on the lump in her throat and came out a whisper.

He wanted to kiss her. She could read the desire in the dark smoky haze of his gaze, but still he hesitated. She lifted her hand to his cheek and guided his lips to hers. She kissed him, softly, tentatively, gently touching his tongue with hers, caressing back and forth, exploring, tasting. As the kiss deepened, she pulled him down closer to her, entwining her arms around his neck and letting herself fall into him.

She loved feeling this close to him, feeling as though for the first time in her life someone was there for her, someone believed in her. She rested her hand on his chest and ran her fingers lightly across his skin, grazing her nails across his collarbone, as her mouth moved longingly over his.

She moaned softly as his lips moved down her neck to nibble at the base of her throat. "Riley," she whispered and inhaled his scent—strong, masculine, protective. Would he protect her? Would he see her through this nightmare when the world began to darken? How far would he go?

Riley drew a quick breath as Devra brushed a soft touch across his chest. Her fingertips feathering his skin sent an electric jolt straight through him. She was beautiful with her long golden curls resting against her shoulders, her lips lush and sensuous, curved in a slight smile. He could see her passion, could feel it, and he had to have her.

He pulled her up against him, his lips falling hard across hers. She wrapped her arms around his neck, pressing her breasts against his chest. He ran the tip of his tongue over the shell of her ear, then drew the little lobe into his mouth. She moaned. His breathing quickened at the deep throaty sound.

She was so sexy and vulnerable and…what? A mystery he couldn't seem to wrap his mind around, a puzzle he just couldn't solve. He lifted her hair and ran his tongue down the column of her throat to play in the grooves of her collarbone. She smelled faintly of vanilla with a touch of desire. She was sweet honey heaven and he couldn't seem to get enough of her.

He lifted her nightshirt. She sat up, her eyes locking on his and helped him pull it over her head. His breath caught in his throat. She was so beautiful. She licked her lips with that sweet little tongue that sent his blood pressure skyrocketing, then moved her hands inside his waistband, undoing whatever control he had left of his senses. If he were making a mistake, it was one more in a long line of them he seemed to be making lately, but he just couldn't help himself. He had to have her, and damn the consequences.

He yanked off his undershorts then pulled her close, loving the feel of her body, her skin against him. His hands moved freely, exploring every inch of her, loving all the little noises she made in response to his kisses, loving the way her body moved beneath his touch. He moved his hand over her most private place. She took a deep startled breath and clutched his shoulders, her nails scratching his slick skin.

"Riley," she moaned.

"Are you sure?" he asked.

She nodded and licked her lips. "Please?"

She didn't need to ask him twice. As the heat within him approached the boiling point, he pulled her legs around his waist, buried his face in her neck, then eased himself inside her.

"Oh," she gasped, then released a whimper of pleasure as he started to move.

Her warm velvety softness encased him. Nothing held him back. He plunged deep inside her. She hung tightly to his neck, pumping her hips, searching for that sweet release. "You feel so good," he groaned. He felt his control slipping away. "Come on, darlin'. Take me home."

He tilted his hips forward, trying to reach the spot that would send her over the edge. She was close; he could feel her teetering on the brink. He took a deep breath and hammered quick, hard thrusts. She stiffened, then cried out, her body shuddering beneath his grasp. Her muscles pulsating around him, she pulled him up, then plunged him down into his own release. When he resurfaced and regained his equilibrium, he took a deep breath, then let it out again. "Lord, have mercy."

DEVRA HAD BEEN dreaming again, she could tell by her hammering heart and quickened breath, but this time she could remember none of it. She turned and watched Riley sleeping soundly. She felt special as the warmth of his touch still permeated her skin. For the first time in her life, she felt as though she wasn't alone. And at the same time, she was never more afraid.

She closed her eyes and pushed back at the fear that her happiness was only temporary. That disaster was only a car ride away. Soon they'd be in Washington and everything would be different. She'd no longer be Devra Morgan. Instead she'd be Devra Miller—the crazy girl with a secret.

She couldn't help wondering how her parents would react to their arrival. The last time she'd seen them, they'd left her at the institution. She'd been thirteen and so scared. They'd never sent for her. Not even during the long Christmas holidays. They'd just locked her up and forgotten her. How could she face them again after that?

She couldn't. They didn't deserve to see her happy, to know she'd gotten out of that horrible place and made a life for herself without them. Bitter tears filled her eyes. Who was she fooling? She missed them. She wanted them to accept her back into their lives, to be proud of her. But could she let them, even if they wanted to?

She climbed out of bed, entered the bathroom and stepped into the shower, letting the hot water rinse away the tears and ease the swelling in her eyes. It would be different this time. They wouldn't reject her again, but even as she told herself the lie, she knew nothing had changed.

"Good morning, doll," Riley said, and reached into the shower to give her a quick kiss.

Of course, things had changed, she thought as she looked into his handsome face. Now she had someone who believed in her, someone who was going to save her from the devil himself. "And that it is," she said with a genuine smile.

THIRTY MINUTES LATER, feeling more contented than she'd ever thought possible, Devra went to the lobby to load up on muffins and fruit from the breakfast buffet for the drive. She'd left Riley singing in the shower and as happy as a lark. She knew she was setting herself up for a fall, but chose to ignore the warnings her subconscious kept sending her. She was determined to hang on to whatever happiness she could while she was still lucky enough to have it.

She took her time choosing from the substantial display of breakfast food and made herself a strong cup of tea. She wasn't looking forward to another long day in the car, even if it was with Riley. With her hands full, she walked back toward the first-floor room, hoping Riley would open the door before she reached it.

"Riley," she called softly as she approached. She glanced to her right into the parking lot to see if he'd started loading their bags into the car, then stopped, unable to comprehend what she was seeing. Riley's car...so much blood. Her breath caught in her throat, her legs weakened beneath her. The cardboard tray of tea, muffins and fruit slipped from her grasp and landed on the ground at her feet. A small sound escaped from her and grew in intensity.

Riley opened the motel door. She looked at him through tears swimming in her eyes, then looked back at his Expedition where something thick and red had been smeared all over his windshield. But as she looked again, she realized it wasn't blood. It was berries…red raspberries.

"Devra, what is it?" Riley rushed toward her, then followed her gaze to the parking lot.

"He's here, Riley. He's found me again. How could he know we're here?" She heard her voice rising with hysteria, but could do nothing to stop it.

"It's okay," Riley said softly and placed a gentle touch on her arm.

"No, it's not okay. How can it be okay? He's been watching us. Every step we've made, he's been right there. He can't be real, Riley. He can't be human. He's coming after me and there isn't anything I can do about it."

Riley seized her shoulders and shook her. "Stop it, Devra."

"No. I can't. I won't. We have to get out of here, but there's no where we can go."

"You're safe. You're with me now. We're going to stop him. Together."

"Don't you get it? We can't stop him. He's a phantom, a *demon*."

He pulled her against him, holding her close. "Devra, he's just a man."

She buried her head in his chest. "There's nowhere I can go, nowhere I can hide. He always finds me."

"Exactly. And that's why you're not going to hide anymore." He pulled her chin up until her eyes locked onto his. "Do you understand? You're not running and you're not hiding. You're going to find out who he is and you're going to take back the life that he stole from you. He's not a devil or a demon. He's just a man. A sick man. Get it?"

She nodded. But he was wrong. There was nothing they could do to stop him. She knew that deep down in her soul.

THE NEXT DAY, Devra sat quietly as they crossed the Columbia River into Washington State. Everything was damp and green, the air cool and crisp. She opened her window and breathed deep the pine-scented air as a flood of memories washed over her. Her heart ached as she thought about her parents and how much she missed them. Would they welcome her home?

She guided Riley off the main freeway and onto the back highways that meandered through the Cascade mountain range.

"Sure is beautiful up here," Riley commented.

"When the sun shines, it's the most beautiful spot on Earth."

"Are you nervous about seeing your parents again?"

She wondered how much it showed. "A little, it's been almost fifteen years."

Confusion played across his face. "Don't you mean ten? Fifteen would have made you too young."

Devra stared out the window trying to come up with an answer that wouldn't have him asking more questions. But he was right, she'd been too young—too young to be forced out of her home. Even after everything they'd been through together, she wondered how he would feel about her once she'd finally worked up the nerve to tell him the truth. She had to. It was only a matter of time before he'd discover it on his own.

"What are your folks like?" he asked.

"I don't know. Normal, small-town religious folks."

"Who think their daughter is a killer?"

"Yeah," she said sadly.

"Maybe they've gotten over it, changed their minds. Time does heal." A dark shadow crossed his eyes.

Not always.

Two hours later, they pulled into a long gravel driveway sculpted out of the forest and curving around massive pines to end at the doorstep of a tiny clapboard house. Devra's throat tightened as she stared at her childhood home. "It looks exactly the same."

Her gaze followed the flight of a dragonfly as it flitted to and fro before disappearing within the green depths of the forest. She had forgotten how surreal and enchanted the forest was. How she'd loved to wander through it, following the fairy trails of butterflies as they zoomed through the thick green ferns.

Wild yellow daisies grew in abundance around the house. As she stared at them, her wonderment and excitement vanished under a heavy cloak of foreboding. He'd been here, her devil. He knew about her childhood field of daisies. Knew how she had liked to pick them to brighten the house. He wanted to remind her. "He wanted me to come home. That's what the daisies were about. That's why he didn't kill me at your ranch." The certain knowledge gripped her heart and squeezed. She'd played right into his deadly hands.

Riley looked confused. "But why?"

"Because it's my turn," she said softly. "The game is up." Something nagged the back of her mind, something she couldn't quite grasp.

"Devra?"

She turned to Riley, but he faded in and out of focus. Laughter rang in her mind—evil, tinny.

"Are you all right?"

The light pressure of his touch on her hand brought her back to the moment, back to him.

She nodded.

The screen door opened and her mother stepped onto the porch, her dark hair pulled severely back from her face, her dull gray dress accented by a frilly white apron. Devra sucked in a breath.

Her mother emitted a soft cry, her hand flying up to cover her mouth. Then she was running toward them. "Devy!" she called. "Papa, Devy's home."

Devra couldn't move. She sat frozen, then the spell broke. Energy surged through her as she fumbled to open the door. She all but fell out of the truck and into her mother's arms. "Mama!" she cried.

Her mother squeezed her tight, rocking her back and forth. "Here, let me have a look at you," she said, drawing back. She smiled and patted down Devra's hair. "Oh, this hair! It's still as wild and troublesome as I remember."

Devra smiled and hugged her mother again. "I've missed you, Mama."

"Not as much as I've missed you, my sweet, sweet child."

Devra breathed deep her mother's familiar scent and her heart filled with sorrow for all the lost days.

A movement on the porch caught her attention. "Papa," she whispered. The last fifteen years had taken their toll on him. He was thicker around the middle and didn't stand quite as straight or as tall as she remembered. The heavy lines on his face decimated the light-hearted, happy man who used to play her handsome prince, rescuing her from the evil queen who lived in the forest.

Tears burned the backs of her eyes.

"Come see your papa. He's missed you." Her mama's words caught and suddenly Devra regretted staying away so long. With their arms clasped around each other's waists, they walked toward the house.

"Hello, Papa," she greeted with a genuine smile and open heart. He stared at her for a long moment, his steely blue eyes assessing her. She stood strong before him while he made up his mind if he would accept her back into his home. He pulled open the screen door and held it ajar.

"Welcome home," he grunted, and behind the hard lines on his face she could see the sadness buried deep in his eyes. She stepped into the circle of his arms and held on tight. "I missed you, Papa." She turned at the sound of the car door closing and smiled as Riley joined them on the porch.

"Mama, Papa, this is my good friend, Riley MacIntyre. And Riley, these are my parents, William and Lydia Miller."

Riley held out his hand, first shaking her father's, then her mother's. "It's nice to meet you," he said.

"Likewise," Lydia said, smiling. "Please, come in and get yourselves something to eat and drink. Where have you come from anyway? Was it far?" she asked as she led them through the small family room and into the kitchen.

"Louisiana," William grunted.

Devra looked up surprised. "How did you know that?"

"License plates."

She smiled. "Of course."

"Louisiana. My, that's a long way," her mother announced as she took a jug of lemonade out of the refrigerator. "We were just sitting down to lunch. How about some chicken soup?"

"With spinach and meatballs?" Devra asked.

"Of course! Here, let me get you a bowl."

Devra caught Riley's eye and smiled as her mother placed large steaming bowls of soup and freshly grated Parmesan cheese in front of them.

"Now eat up. Both of you."

Devra put the spoon to her lips and savored the hearty broth. It had been so long since she'd had her mother's cooking, or anything remotely resembling it. She looked around the kitchen, soaking up the yellow tiles, the ceramic kitten cookie jar, the small milk glass vase on the table. All these things and so much more were exactly as they had been before, as if the earth had sucked her in and sent her cascading down a time warp into her past when she'd been ten years old and hadn't a care in the world.

Except Riley was sitting next to her, watching her with speculative eyes.

"Thank you, Mama," she said softly and sipped another spoonful of soup.

"Tell us what you've been doing. How did you end up all the way down in Louisiana?" she asked, her eyes bright with curiosity.

"I move around a lot."

"Why is that?" her papa asked, breaking his silence.

She didn't know how to answer him.

"You came home for a reason, didn't you, Devy?" His voice, deep and penetrating, touched her like no other could. He always seemed to be able to see inside her mind, to know what she was thinking. Why hadn't he been able to see the truth, that she hadn't killed Tommy? *That she wasn't sick?*

After that horrible day, she hadn't been able to do anything to please him. As if she'd been damaged in some way. On that count, she supposed he was right. She had been damaged, and she still was. The negative thoughts churned away inside her, bringing with them fatigue and sorrow.

"I came home hoping you would help me." Her eyes locked on his. She'd always believed if she could only have made it home that day, he would have helped her, he would have saved her. But she hadn't been able to find her way. She was home now, but she couldn't be sure if he'd be able to help her, and she knew for certain that no one could save her. Not even Riley.

He was coming, and there was nothing any of them could do to stop him.

Chapter Twelve

Devra stood at her mama's kitchen window and stared into the forest she'd loved to play in as a child. She tried to peer through the thick green plants and oversize ferns, past the trees covered with moss, but she couldn't see ten feet into the forest. Anyone could be out there…watching. Waiting.

"Devy, come back to the table and finish your soup," her mama insisted as if nothing were wrong, as if they hadn't been out of her life for fifteen years. She looked to her papa, then back to her mama again. How long would they sit there acting as if nothing had happened? Acting as if they hadn't tossed her away, never to be thought of again. Devra sat down, unsure how to broach the subject that brought them there.

Riley took her hand and gave it a squeeze. "That sure was wonderful soup, Mrs. Miller."

"Thank you," she said, smiling. "Devra used to help me make it all the time, before…"

Before you sent me away?

She wanted to ask them why they'd done it, demand

answers. But she couldn't, not while Riley was there. She wasn't ready for him to know she'd spent five years in a mental institution. She didn't want him to look at her like her papa did, as if she were crazy.

Her mama's cheeks flushed. "What do you do for work? How do you make your living? Tell me everything about your life, Devy."

"I need to find out what happened to Tommy, Mama. That's why I'm here."

Her mama scoffed and looked away. "We don't need to bring all that up again. That poor child. God rest his soul."

"We do need to bring it up again. The man who killed him…he's back. He's coming for me."

Her mother's face turned ashen. Her grasp on her lemonade glass tightened as her hands began to tremble.

"I know you didn't believe me," Devra continued, pushing forward even though she could see her mother's distress. "After a while, I wasn't sure I believed me either. When I left—" she glanced at Riley, who gave her an encouraging nod "—that is, when I moved to Seattle, I attended college and tried to make a life for myself. But it happened again, a woman was killed. I moved to Portland, then San Francisco, Miami and finally New Orleans. Everywhere I went, I dreamed of death. And all the women in my dreams were killed."

"Please, Devy, I can't go through all that again. I just can't. They're the devil's work, these dreams."

"Enough!" her papa roared, and grasped the table so hard the tablecloth bunched beneath his fingers.

Devra stared at him, refusing to yield. "The man who killed Tommy follows me everywhere I go. He kills people. Now he's after me." She picked up a daisy out of the milk glass vase and threw it on the table. "He leaves me messages. My only chance to beat him is to find out the truth about what happened here fifteen years ago. About what happened to Tommy, before it happens to me."

Her parents looked at each other, a silent message passing between them.

"How dare you come here and speak to your mama and me about such things? After everything we did for you, after all you put us through."

"Papa, please." Lydia stood and rushed to her husband. "You're turning all red. It's not good for you. You know what the doctor said."

"What doctor?" Devra asked, as fear for his health grabbed hold of her heart. "What's wrong?"

Fire burned deep in his eyes. "You tell him the truth, Devra Ann." He gestured toward Riley. "You tell him what a sweet child you were, the light of your mama's and my life."

Her mother dropped her head into her hand.

"Do you think we wanted to believe our daughter was sick?"

Devra cringed at her papa's words.

"But things started happening around here—the gas left on, the lug nuts loosened on my car. You claimed it wasn't you, but I found the tire iron in your room."

"It wasn't me. Why would I want to hurt you?" Dread clutched her heart and sickened her. Had the killer been trying to hurt her family? She turned to Riley. He had that cold, wary cop's expression on his face. She didn't like it. He had to believe in her. She wouldn't have the strength to continue without him. To fight this battle alone.

"The year you turned thirteen, puberty and the devil struck and stole that sweet child right out of our lives."

"Please, William. Don't bring all that back up again. I can't bear it."

"We have to, Lydia. Don't you see? It's happening again. She's come back because more have died. Death follows her like stink on a skunk. I tried to cleanse her of it, but she's come and brought the devil back home."

Tears filled Devra's eyes. She loved her papa with all her heart, even after all he'd done to "cleanse" her of the devil: the scrubbings with the hard boar brush, the nightly Bible readings until her eyes burned with fatigue. But she knew it had come from his heart. She had tried to understand until he sent her away.

"We brought you back after Tommy died," her papa continued. "We were determined to fight for you, to fight for your freedom, but then the dreams came. They were brutal. You wrote them down in your diary and your mama found it. Horrific things no young sweet child would even imagine, let alone write. They say puberty does strange things to the mind but we never imagined…"

"We had to send you away. It broke our hearts, but what choice did we have?" Lydia pleaded for understanding.

"There was something very wrong with you. I guess there were signs earlier. There was a kitten once…but you were always such an angel, inside and out."

Devra couldn't move. Resentment blurred her vision. "I loved that kitten. I never would have—" She couldn't even say the words, couldn't even let her mind flash back to what had been done to her beloved pet. "You really, honestly believed that I was capable of such violence? You are my parents. You raised me. You are supposed to be my advocate, to believe in me when no one else does, to protect me. Instead, you fed me to the wolves."

Her head was spinning. Tears were closing her throat and threatening to overwhelm her. She wouldn't get help here. She had been a fool to think she would. She rose from the table and turned toward the door.

"Paranoid delusions. Schizophrenic. Withdrawn."

She stopped and turned back to her father. Fear commingled with dread and choked any words she might have spoken to stop him.

"Those are just a few of the words the doctors at the sanitarium used to describe your condition. They said they could cure you. They said they could make you better. How could they have let you out, if they'd been so wrong? If more people have had to die? God help me."

Devra stood rooted to the floor, her eyes focused on Riley's. He stared at her, with what? Hurt? Confusion? Disgust? She should have told him. She knew the truth would come out. She had only prayed it wouldn't have.

"I wasn't sick." Her voice shook as she said the words. Years of pent-up anger and frustration overwhelmed her. She couldn't think, couldn't breathe, could only feel. "You locked me up in that horrible place and never came to see me. Not once. If you had,

I could have told you the truth. I could have told you that I wasn't sick. I didn't need all the drugs those so-called doctors were drowning me with."

She took a step toward them. "Not that it would have mattered. Not that you would have believed me. I didn't kill Tommy. I didn't deserve to be locked up." Her voice broke with emotion. "I didn't deserve to lose my family. You were all I had in the world. And you turned your backs on me."

Her mama looked at her with years of pain and regret distorting her face. Devra couldn't swallow. Bitterness filled her father's face. Shocked disbelief filled Riley's.

"I was a child, a little girl." Not able to bear any more, she turned from them and left the room, running out the door and into the woods, hoping to get as far away from them as she could. Riley's shocked expression flashed painfully through her mind. He was as lost to her as her parents were. Now he knew the truth. He knew there was something wrong with her. He knew she wasn't worthy of his love. How could she be? She was damaged.

RILEY WAS STILL TRYING to process what Devra's father had said when Devra ran out the door. He jumped up. "Devra, wait!" he called.

"Don't worry," her father said. "She knows that forest like the back of her hand. She just needs a few minutes."

Riley stared at him. "Don't you understand? She wasn't exaggerating. There is a killer after her."

"No, Son, there isn't. That's what you have failed to understand. It's her. It's always been her." William shook his head.

His words wrenched loose a deep fear in Riley. No, it wasn't possible. "Someone has been stalking her, things have happened."

"Things she could have done on her own?"

Riley thought back to the raspberries smeared across his windshield and the way she disappeared that day when he was in the tree house. He supposed she could have done it. "No. I was attacked at my house." And there was a man at the hospital speaking with Nurse Jenkins, the man who had Devra's locket.

"I don't have all the answers for you," William said. "I only know what happened here."

"But you had your own daughter committed to a sanitarium?"

William leaned back in his chair, his eyes hard, his tone cold. "Don't pass judgment on us. You weren't here. You didn't see what she'd done to that poor boy. You didn't see the state she was in afterward."

Lydia swiped the tears from her cheeks. "We've always done what we thought was best for Devy. That's all, nothing less, nothing more." She rose to clear the table.

Riley tried to understand, but he just couldn't get past the image of Devra thirteen years old and locked in an institution. No wonder she kept herself isolated from people. No wonder she couldn't trust.

Riley stood. "There wasn't enough evidence to prove she killed that boy. They released her back to you, back into your care."

"That's right. And that's when her nightmares started. Terrible dreams that would have her sitting up in bed at night, screaming loud enough to wake the dead. Her head full of disgusting visions straight from hell itself. Chief Marshall would come by every few days to check on things, to harass us because we still had our child, while his was buried down at Pearson's Cemetery."

Riley looked him square in the eye. "She didn't do it. If you have any information about what did happen here fifteen years ago, please, help us. Help her."

William paused and suddenly the years of pain and suffering showed in every line on his face, each fold of his skin, and Riley knew this man had endured more than any man should ever have to bear.

"My daughter isn't right in the head, son. You heard what she said about the others. Where she goes, death follows. She can't help it, she was born that way."

Riley had heard enough. There wasn't any more any of them could do here. "I feel sorry for you, Mr. Miller. Devra is a warm, caring person with a big heart. She loves children and she loves animals. She volunteers every week at the Children's Hospital, reading to the kids, helping them through their suffering. She isn't a cold-blooded killer, and she isn't mentally insane. If you knew your daughter at all, you would already know that."

He left the kitchen and followed the path out of the front yard and into the woods, heading toward the river. His head ached and his nerves were fried.

My daughter isn't right in the head, son.

He'd sounded so certain, so sure of himself. *Devra.*

An ache rumbled inside him as her name whispered through his mind. What if he'd made a mistake? What if she really was sick? What if she had to go back to the sanitarium? He closed his eyes, as the image of cold granite and tall iron fences entered his mind. Now he knew why she was so afraid of being locked up. She had been locked up—in a mental institution.

"Devra!" he yelled. The forest swallowed the sound as if it had never been spoken. Riley moved deeper into the shadows. This forest was different than the woods back home—colder, darker. Even the sky above him was a different shade of blue. He felt almost as if he'd stepped into a different reality, one where he was no longer sure of himself, or of her. Suddenly, he wasn't sure of anything.

He heard the roar of the river before the sparkling waters came into view. He saw her sitting on a rock by its bank, her head bent on drawn-up knees. She looked so small, so beautiful, so much in need of his help. He wouldn't let her down.

"Devra," he said softly.

She turned to look at him. The puffy redness circling her eyes broke his heart.

"You okay?"

She sniffed, nodding. "I'm sorry you had to witness that wonderful display of family love."

"I'm sorry you had to grow up with it." He sat down next to her. "I don't know how you did it. How you survived."

She took a deep breath. "Neither do I."

"It's over now. They can't hurt you any longer."

She turned to him, wrapped her arms around his neck and leaned her head against his shoulder. "I wish that were true."

He held her for a moment. "Why didn't you tell me about the sanitarium?"

"I couldn't."

Her simply stated words tore at him. She still didn't trust him.

"I didn't want you to look at me like—like I was *damaged*." The word caught on something in her throat and came out a hoarse whisper.

He squeezed her, holding her a little tighter. "You can trust me, Devra. I hope I've proven that to you."

Something flashed in her eyes and he realized she still didn't trust him, even after all he'd risked for her. Disappointment tightened his chest.

"I'm sorry. I'm just scared."

They sat in silence for a few minutes watching the water tumble over the rocks. "Is this where Tommy was killed?" he asked.

She shook her head. "No, we were deeper in the forest, farther down that way." She pointed upriver.

He nodded. "Is it hard for you to be here?"

"No. The river calms me, it always has. The rushing water soothes my nerves, makes me forget."

He smiled, but couldn't agree. The water's roar was too loud, masking the sound of anything that might be coming.

"What was it like at the sanitarium?"

"Awful. They were told I'd killed Tommy when I had been admitted. I tried to tell them different, but they didn't believe me, especially after they learned about the dreams."

"Like the ones about Michelle and our intruder? You had dreams of people dying back then?"

"Not always, but sometimes. In any case, they were always violent and scary. I didn't understand what they were and no one was able to help me. When I tried to verbalize my fears or talk about my dreams, they medicated me. They said I was delusional and dangerous. I learned to write them down. I had to get the visions out or I really would go insane. I—"

"Shh, you're not insane. You never were." Paranoid delusions. Schizophrenic. Withdrawn. Wasn't that what her father had said? "You shouldn't have kept all this from me. We need to be honest with each other if we're going to beat this guy. We can't keep secrets."

"What could I have said? How could I have convinced you that I hadn't killed your sister-in-law, but I'd dreamed of her death? That I'd once been arrested for murdering a boy even though I'd been innocent? No one believed me. They all thought I was crazy. And, apparently, they still do," she muttered. "Before I could have said psychic connection, you would have locked me up in your fine, upstanding New Orleans jail and have forgotten about me."

"You don't know that."

"Oh, yes, I do. One thing I know about you, Riley MacIntyre, is that you'll do anything for your family. You'll do anything to find Michelle's killer. The fact that you're here with me now risking everything you believe in proves that."

"You're right. I will do anything for my family. And right now, I consider you part of my family. I care for you, and I'm not going to let anything happen to you."

She looked up at him with a wide vulnerable gaze that reached inside and touched his heart.

"I won't let anyone lock you up again, I promise." And he meant it. He would do whatever it took to protect her. To do what her father should have done fifteen years ago, to stand up and fight for her right to have survived the brutality of a madman.

"You might not be able to stop them."

"We'll stop them together. We'll discover the truth and we'll find your devil."

"I wish I could believe you. But the river's talking to me, and it's telling me this isn't going to end well. Disaster's coming, I can feel it with every breath I take, and if I close my eyes I can hear it whispered in the wind."

The coldness in her gaze, the dead certainty shook him.

"Evil's going to win," she whispered. "It always does, and there isn't anything you or I are going to be able to do about it."

Chapter Thirteen

Evil always wins. It certainly had that day in the park when a mugger got too rough and killed his mother. Riley hadn't been able to stop it; he hadn't been able to save her. Evil always wins—it was his biggest fear and what he'd been fighting against his entire life. "You're wrong. I won't be evil's punching bag and neither will you. We're going to fight back. We have to. It's either that or give up and die."

Devra sighed. "You're right. Running and hiding isn't the answer, it isn't living. You taught me that."

He held her close, and looked over her shoulder into the deep pockets of the trees where the light couldn't reach and stifled a quiver of uneasiness, then kissed her. With a little more force, a little more passion to chase away the fear that she was right. Something bad *was* coming.

Rocks crunched beneath steel-toed boots as someone stepped behind them. Devra drew back with a start, her eyes wide. Quickly, Riley turned. William Miller was standing directly behind them, his watery eyes filled with sadness.

"I think it's time you two left."

No goodbyes? Riley didn't know why he was surprised. He stood, pulling Devra up next to him. "I agree. Thank you for your hospitality. And please thank Mrs. Miller, too."

Devra stopped in front of her father. "The devil was here, Papa, only he wasn't inside of me. He's not in my 'blood.' If you can't find it in your heart to see the truth and help me, the devil might just win."

Riley didn't like the surprise that entered her father's eyes, or the certain knowledge that he was hiding something. Something that might just get them killed.

FIFTEEN MINUTES LATER, Devra pointed to the sign that read Rosemont. Trepidation rose within her as she stared at that sign. She shouldn't have come back here. There must be a different way. She knew that every person she saw would look at her and think, "There's that crazy girl, the one who killed Chief Marshall's son." She shuddered. She couldn't go through that again.

Riley slowed the car as signs of civilization came into view. The whole town consisted of maybe five blocks, with restaurants and stores and gas stations on either side of the highway. He stopped in front of Mrs. Hutchinson's Bed and Breakfast. She stared up at the gray Victorian with loads of pink gingerbread trim. It hadn't changed, not one bit.

"I can't stay here," she said softly. "I know this place."

"Looks like we don't have much choice." He pointed

to the abandoned Crazy Eight Motel across the street, where several windows were boarded up and a Closed sign hung haphazardly from one hinge.

"At least no one would know me there."

Riley squeezed her shoulder. "It'll be all right."

She smiled at him, nodded, then reluctantly climbed the front steps. It wouldn't be all right. Nothing had been all right, not for a very long time.

The door chimed as they opened it and walked into the front parlor. The familiar smell of lemon oil assaulted her as they moved deeper into the room, passing polished antique furniture and walking across a worn maroon carpet to a long wooden counter. Her head began to swim and her stomach turned at the heavy lemon smell.

Nothing had changed. The same pictures adorned the walls, the same candy dish sat on the sideboard, and Mr. Peabody… She stopped and stared at the tortoiseshell cat lying in his basket. "It's not possible, is it?"

Riley turned. "What?"

She bent down to touch the cat. Mere inches from his soft fur she stopped herself and quickly straightened. "It's not breathing," she said and took a quick step back.

"Oh, hello, there," a woman said, entering from a back room. "Don't be alarmed. That's Mr. Peabody. I couldn't bear to part with him, so I had him stuffed. Hard to tell, eh?"

Devra stifled a shudder as she looked down at the poor cat. Poor Mr. Peabody, stuck forever in this lemon-scented tomb. She tried to wipe the expression of revulsion off her face before turning back to Mrs.

Hutchinson. Thankfully she had changed, or Devra was sure she'd run from the room, screaming. The woman's hair was now completely gray and cut close to her head, somehow making her appear softer than she remembered.

"We were hoping to get a room for the night," Riley said.

"Of course you are. Why else would you be here?" She turned and selected a key off a brass rack behind her. When she turned again, her smile faltered as her sharp eyes perused Devra's face. "Do I know you?"

"No," Devra lied.

The woman's eyes narrowed.

"We're from Louisiana," Riley added.

"Hmm, still…something about you looks familiar. I never forget a face."

Devra cringed under her scrutiny. If she knew the truth, would she let them stay? Would she call Chief Marshall? Would they tie her to the nearest stake and burn her?

Riley accepted the key she offered. They followed her up the stairs to a quaint room on the third floor, decorated with too many flowers and way too much pink. "I have a cat who's been stuck in the car for days," Devra started.

"There's a greenhouse out back. You can let him roam in there." Mrs. Hutchinson's lips drew tight, as if pulled by an imaginary string. "It's perfectly safe, no predators or man-eating plants, probably just an extra-large rodent or two to keep him company."

Devra arched a brow and shuffled uncomfortably under the woman's narrow gaze.

"We would really appreciate that," Riley said, giving Devra a nod before following the woman back downstairs to unload their bags and get Felix settled in the greenhouse.

Devra parted the lace curtains and stared down at the street below as she tried to relax the tension in her shoulders. From the outside, Rosemont, Washington, was the perfect Americana small town, where everyone knew one another and nothing bad ever happened. But it had. And she had a terrible feeling that now that she was back, it was about to happen again.

She watched the wind kick up and give the tall pines a good shake. The sky darkened as black clouds raced across the sun. A chill raised the hair on her arms and suddenly she knew that her luck was about to run out. Riley stepped behind her and placed his arms around her waist. She leaned back against his chest and sighed.

"Come on, let's lie down," he whispered.

She nodded and followed him to the bed.

He stretched out on his stomach, then turned to look at her. "Do you trust me, Devra?"

She looked into his eyes and saw how open he was to her, how much he wanted to believe. "Yes," she said softly. "I trust you. I trust you with my life." *It's my heart I'm not so sure about.*

"Any more secrets?"

She stared at him. "There are so many things…. I've been afraid for so long."

He pulled her next to him and within minutes she

drifted asleep with his warm smell offering a comfort she knew was only temporary. Secrets… There were so many.

HE WALKED SLOWLY through the woods, following a narrow path that looked as if the forest had almost succeeded in reclaiming it into its fold. He stepped around a massive tree and the house came into view. It was a small house badly in need of repairs. The siding had come off in places and several of the windows were boarded up or broken where the boards were missing.

He was humming, a familiar tune that nagged the back of her mind. An overwhelming sense of fear flooded through her. It entered her mouth, her ears, her lungs. She couldn't breathe.

Please, don't go near the house!

She tried to run, but couldn't. The tune danced across her mind. A sick, torturous melody—somehow distorted, somehow wrong.

The boards had been removed from the front door. He reached out his hand and turned the knob.

"No!" her mind screamed.

The door swung open.

She saw the room as it was before—hardwood floors gleaming, a round rug that she knew would feel rough beneath her hands and knees. Her vision blurred and suddenly she could see him placing daisies in a dirty glass on a warped table. The rug was gone, the floor splintered and beyond repair.

"Daisies for my Devy," he whispered.

Her throat tightened. He picked up the glass with the

flowers and turned toward the kitchen. As he walked, she thought she saw him stepping in something on the floor. What was it?

Pain erupted in her chest. It hurt. She wanted to cry, to scream.

Blood. There was so much blood.

Mama!

A strangled cry erupted from Devra's throat. She sat straight up, coughing, unable to catch her breath.

"Devra, what is it? What's wrong?"

She turned to Riley, unable to comprehend the horror of her dream or the certain knowledge that it was more: a premonition, a memory?

"You're so pale," Riley said, pulling her into his arms and rubbing her back.

But it was no use. She couldn't feel him. She could only feel the sensation of ice-cold water rolling over her skin, could only see a large puddle of blood spreading slowly across a golden floor, could only hear the simple tune from a child's music box playing over and over in her mind.

"Devra, you're scaring me. What is it?"

His tone, his rough shake pulled her from the last vestiges of her dream. She stared at him, her eyes locking onto his. "I don't know," she whispered.

"Bad dream?"

She nodded and could see that he wanted more. But she couldn't give it to him. She didn't know how. "I...I think I'm going to drown."

Alarm filled his face. "Why?"

"I don't know. I'm just so cold. I can feel the water, can taste it."

"Okay," he said and pulled her close. "It's going to be all right. You're going to be all right." After a few minutes the warmth returned to her skin.

"Can you tell me anything more?"

She shook her head. "Nothing that makes any sense, sorry."

"It's okay. I'm here now. You don't have to face this alone. We'll get through this thing."

She nodded, though she could see the lie in his eyes. He was scared, and not just of her devil. He was worried her father was right about her. He was looking at her as if she might have to go back to the sanitarium and that he would have to be the one to send her there.

"You think you're up to seeing Chief Marshall?" he asked.

She shook her head. She would never be up to facing the chief, to looking into those cold, hate-filled eyes. But she knew she couldn't avoid him, she knew she'd have to face him if she wanted to live. Because one thing was certain—her time was almost up. "No, but I will," she said, and changed into a chambray peasant skirt that flared around her legs and a long-sleeved white blouse.

"Feeling better?" Riley asked when she was dressed and ready to go.

Devra nodded, though she couldn't shake the trepidation squeezing her heart. Even though Riley was by her side, suddenly she felt very alone. She wouldn't be facing the chief with her lover, she'd be facing him with another cop. And even though the chief didn't have anything to hold her on, the irrational fear that once she walked through his doors she wouldn't walk out again was overwhelming.

She shook it off, and got into the car next to Riley. She had to make the most of this visit, because finding out who killed Tommy was her only hope. Within minutes, Riley parked the car in front of the small courthouse building. "I'll be right by your side," he whispered and squeezed her hand.

She smiled as she looked at him and wished she could count on that, but something inside her whispered his support would be short-lived. He was a cop after all, and they were walking into cop territory—into Chief Marshall's territory.

A few people sitting here and there in large vinyl chairs looked up as they walked into the station. The reception area was pleasant, with lots of windows, ferns and comfy chairs. Unfortunately, the decor was lost on her.

A woman Devra's age sat behind the large counter. "Hello, can I help you?"

"That's all right, Mandy," Chief Marshall said as he walked into the room. "They're here to see me."

Startled by his voice, Devra looked up.

"Heard you were back, I was just getting ready to hunt you down."

She stared at the man who'd haunted too many of her sleepless nights. On the surface, he had a kind face with a hint of gray at his temples and soft gray eyes. But she knew looks could be deceiving. She knew how that face could darken with hate. "I've forgotten how fast news spreads in a small town."

He grunted. "I'm sure you have."

Riley held out his hand. "Chief Marshall? I'm Detective Riley MacIntyre from the New Orleans Police Department."

The chief showed only a second of surprise before the aloof veneer dropped back over his face. He studied Riley for a minute, then took his hand. "Why don't the two of you come on into my office? We have some things we need to discuss."

Devra followed him, trying not to let the panic rising within her gain hold. She glanced back behind her at the few people sitting in the reception area. They were staring at her with curiosity alive in their eyes. Soon they'd be whispering about how they saw the woman who'd killed the chief's son.

She turned away from them and watched the chief walk ahead of her. How had he known she was back so fast? Had her parents called him? Had they told him what she'd said about the others? The feeling of betrayal ate at her.

They entered the chief's office and sat in the chairs in front of his desk.

"I'll have to ask you to hang your piece there by the door," the chief said to Riley.

Devra looked up in surprise. She hadn't been aware Riley had his gun. Riley nodded and hung his jacket on the coat tree by the door, then removed his shoulder holster and placed it on top of the jacket.

Chief Marshall nodded but didn't speak, just opened

his drawer and pulled out a thick file with her name on it. Devra took a deep breath to steady herself and tried not to think about what that file might contain, or how many years he'd spent working on it.

Looking away from the file, she saw a picture of Tommy on his desk. Memories flooded her mind—his smile, his laugh, the twinkle in his eyes as he'd chase her through the forest. He'd been her best friend, her first crush. She'd loved Tommy. Yet she'd never been allowed to mourn him, to go to his funeral, to say goodbye. This man stole that from her, that and so much more.

She fought the despair filling her heart and turned to Riley. He reached out his hand. She took it and gave him a grateful smile.

"You've been quite a busy woman over the years, Devra."

"Have I?" she asked, and turned to look at the chief, to face the coldness in his eyes.

"I had a hard time tracking you down at first, once you changed your name."

A band tightened around her chest.

"It took me quite a few years to discover how you could be making a living, paying taxes, being an up-standing citizen of a community, when it seemed Devra Miller had dropped off the face of the earth. In fact, you have quite a few secrets, don't you, Ms. Miller?"

Secrets.

She glanced at Riley and gnawed the corner of her lip. "I—I didn't kill Tommy. That's why we're here. We want to discover the truth."

"Which truth would that be? That you're not Devra

Morgan? Or that you're not D. M. Miller? The author who writes stories of gruesome murders, stories that are suspiciously close to murders that have actually taken place." He sat back in his chair, a Cheshire cat grin splitting his face.

Paralyzing dread grabbed hold and turned her stomach.

"You're D. M. Miller?" The accusation in Riley's tone cut her to the quick.

Chief Marshall swiveled his chair around to the bookshelf behind him and pulled down several books, all by D. M. Miller, all books Riley had heard of. In fact, Michelle had been a big fan. He recalled the typed pages he'd found in Devra's printer describing Michelle's death. Would his sister-in-law's last moments end up in Devra's next book? The thought sickened him.

"Have you read any?" the chief asked.

Riley shook his head. He'd always meant to, just never found the time.

"Fascinating stuff, plots are captivating, compelling. I'm sure it won't be long before she hits the bestseller list."

"How'd you find out?" Devra squeaked.

"What do you suppose your publishers would think if they found out your stories were based on actual cases? Or how will your fans feel if they find out you spent five years in a mental institution?"

Riley had heard enough. He dropped Devra's hand and leaned forward. "I don't see how any of this is relevant to why we're here." He cut in, disgusted by the chief's smugness, disgusted that the man would throw her time in the institution back in her face, and disgusted with himself for believing all the secrets were out, that there couldn't possibly be anything else Devra was keeping from him.

"Don't you?" the chief asked. "Well that's because you've never read one of her books. Here, let me save you the trouble. Book number one—*A Time to Die.*" He held up the first book. "Our heroine is trying to discover the identity of a serial killer. She doesn't. Nor does she in books two and three, but that's okay, there's plenty of other mischief going on that she does figure out. It's a great plot device, drawing the readers back, again and again, to discover who the killer can be. But what brings me back are the victims. Here, I've made it easy for you."

He pulled a yellow pad out of the file. "Victim number one, killed in Seattle. Victim number two, killed in Portland. Victim number three, killed in Miami. Ringing any bells yet?"

Riley stiffened, a cold dread working its way through his system.

"All blond, all have long, curly hair, all blue eyes. In fact, the specific details to the real victims in each of those cities are startlingly close, so close one would have to conclude that she's very good at her research. Except for one small detail."

Riley frowned.

"Each victim in her stories was left posed with their pinkies intertwined together."

Riley felt the color drain from his face as the image of Michelle propped against the wall, her hands resting in her lap, her pinkies interlaced came to the forefront of his mind.

"Yep, thought it would sound familiar to you. Just like that young woman killed down there round your parts."

Riley pushed back his chair and stood. He rubbed a palm across his face and leaned back against the wall.

Devra couldn't breathe. The chief had her, dead to rights, and soon Riley would look at her the way the chief was looking at her. As if she were a monster. As if everything she'd ever said to him, everything she'd felt for him was a lie.

"It's a detail that wouldn't mean very much, except that was the one detail the police hadn't released to the papers. So, what I'd like to know, little girl—" Marshall leaned forward across his desk and pinned her to the chair with his cold, hard eyes "—is exactly how you gleaned that little bit of information from those crime scenes."

"You wouldn't believe me if I told you."

"She's psychic," Riley answered bluntly. His hair was spiked back from running his fingers through it, and a defeated look had settled on his face. But he hadn't given up on her, not yet.

Chief Marshall snorted. "And you believe that?"

"Yes, sir, I do. And I also believe the man who killed Michelle…that is, the man who killed the woman in New Orleans, intends to kill Miss Morgan—" he shook his head as if to clear it "—Miss Miller next."

Chief Marshall leaned back in his chair. "That's very interesting. Psychic, you say." He twiddled with the pencil on his desk, while his eyes bored through her.

"I've spent the last fifteen years compiling this file. In fact, you could say it's become my life's work to know everything there is to know about you, to enter the mind of a female serial killer."

"I am not a killer." She stated the fact coolly.

He waved a dismissive hand. "There's just one thing I've never been able to determine, and no matter how many times I've asked your folks, they won't tell me."

Riley stood in the corner, staring at both of them, not saying a word, his face void of expression.

Devra let out a deep breath. "All right, I'll play. What?"

"How'd you break your right pinky?"

Confused, she stared at him, then looked down at her hand. "What are you talking about?"

"I have your medical records right here and, apparently, at age thirty-six months, you were brought in to Dr. Carleen to have your right pinky examined. It had been broken and set somewhere else, but Mrs. Miller wanted him to do the follow-up visit. So I'd like to know, how'd you break your pinky?"

"How on earth would I know that? I didn't even know it had been broken." She stared again at her hand. All her fingers looked fine. Was he jesting? Trying to trip her up? "I'm sure my parents would have told me if I'd broken my pinky, Chief Marshall. I believe you are mistaken."

"Nope, says right here. Office visit for examination of broken small finger on patient's right hand. Couldn't get your parents to remember anything about it either."

"Well, obviously, there's been some mistake, because I'm sure my mother would remember if I'd broken my finger."

He nodded. "I'm sure you're right. Which got me thinking, why would they lie? What are they trying to hide? Then it occurred to me that maybe they're not your parents after all."

"What? That's absurd." She looked to Riley.

"Is it? There's no birth certificate on file for Devra Miller anywhere in King County. Yet your parents claimed they moved here with you from Evergreen when you were three. In fact, they moved to town right before your visit to Dr. Carleen. So I decided to do a little investigating, and would you believe no one remembers the Millers in Evergreen giving birth to a baby girl. Not a soul. I sure find that mighty strange."

"What are you saying?" Disbelief coursed through her. It couldn't be. Then a smaller voice, a stronger voice asked, "Then why did they send you away? Maybe they didn't want you. Maybe you aren't theirs."

She stood, and grabbed the back of the chair. Sickness churned in her stomach. "I need to use the rest room."

"Right down the hall to the left."

Devra opened the door and flew down the hall.

Chief Marshall followed her flight. "She's not psychic, Mr. MacIntyre. That little girl is a fruitcake, had been when she killed my boy, was when she'd been up there in that institution. What we have here is a sick little serial killer." His determined tone almost sounded sad.

The weight of a hundred worlds rested on Riley's shoulders. "I need to make a few calls."

Chapter Fourteen

Devra stared at herself in the bathroom mirror of the Rosemont Police Department and splashed cold water on her face, trying to fight back the nausea rising in her throat. Chief Marshall was going to send her back to the sanitarium. He was obsessed with her, and he wouldn't stop until she was locked up for good.

Tears filled her eyes and spilled onto her cheeks. Even Riley was beginning to doubt her. She could see it in his eyes, and that, more than anything else, was breaking her heart. How could she live through the abandonment again? Through the loneliness and pain of realizing there was no one out there who cared about her? How could they? She was a monster. But it wasn't her. Why couldn't they see that?

The chief's words played over and over in her mind. *No birth certificate on file anywhere in King County.* Her parents had always lived in Rosemont, at least, that's what she'd been led to believe. Apparently, she'd been wrong.

They're not your parents. That's why they gave you

up. That's why they don't care. The thoughts ran through her mind, twisting, turning, torturing her until she thought she'd scream. Who was she?

She wasn't a killer, she knew that. And nothing could convince her she had killed Tommy or anyone else. Her parents, or whoever they were, had a lot of questions to answer and this time she wouldn't let them off so easy.

She stepped into the hall and glanced into the chief's office. No one was there. Where had they gone? *To prepare her a padded cell?* Not this time. Not ever again.

She spotted Riley's jacket and holster hanging inside the door. She grabbed his keys out of his pocket and, after a second's hesitation, took his gun. She could no longer count on him to protect her. He had his doubts, she could read them clearly in his eyes, and those doubts could get them killed. From here on out, she was on her own.

She slipped the gun into the pocket of her skirt, then shifted the waistband so it wouldn't show as the gun's weight pulled on the loose fabric. She heard the chief's voice down the hall, turned, and quickly walked toward the reception area.

"Are you leaving, Miss Miller?" Mandy asked from behind the counter of the receptionist's station.

Devra forced a wide, friendly smile onto her face. "Just for a minute, I left something back at the hotel I'd like the chief to see. I'll be right back."

Mandy nodded, picked up her coffee cup and waved it at her. "All righty then, see you soon," she said and headed down the hall.

Expelling a relieved sigh, Devra forced herself to act casual and walk slowly out the door.

RILEY SAT in the conference room and stared at his phone. How much of a coincidence was it that all the victims had their pinkies interlaced and Devra had had hers broken? Where was his gut instinct? Why didn't he just know what the truth was? He turned on his phone and called Mac, wanting to check in at home to see if anything else had happened while he'd been gone.

"Where have you been?" his brother, Mac, asked after answering the phone. He still sounded mad and Riley supposed he would be for a long time.

"I've been out of town, dealing with a few things."

"You missed Michelle's funeral."

Pain and dread squeezed Riley's heart, making him gasp. "Oh, no. I'm sorry. I…" What could he possibly say? That he'd forgotten? It had slipped his mind? He'd been too busy chasing phantom demons and falling in love?

"I thought Michelle meant something to you," Mac said, emotion straining his voice.

Riley rubbed his face. "I know you want to blame me. Do it, blame me. If it will make you feel better. I should have paid more attention. I should have watched her better. If only I'd been more—"

"Protective?"

Riley gave a bitter laugh. "Yes, protective. She needed it, Mom needed it and now Devra needs it, and I seem to be letting them all down. And for that, we've all been paying the price."

"Do you think you could be any more arrogant? My happiness, Michelle's happiness, did not weigh on your shoulders. We would have been perfectly fine, perfectly happy without you. In fact—"

"In fact, if I weren't around, Mom wouldn't have gone looking for me at the park and gotten killed, and I wouldn't have become a cop, and Michelle wouldn't have followed me onto the force…." Riley couldn't say another word, his throat was blocked with emotion.

"I was going to say in fact, we are all responsible for the decisions we make, good or bad. Don't take *that* away from us, too. And if you still don't get it, then there really isn't anything that can be said." Mac paused. "Why is there a drawing of John Miller in your kitchen?"

Riley tightened his grasp on the phone. "The police sketch? You know him?"

"He's a friend from work. Michelle and I had him over for dinner a few weeks ago. What's this all about?"

Did he know about me? About Mom? That would explain the picture in the tree house. The killer was playing with him, playing with them all. "Mac, do me a favor and take the sketch to Tony. Tell him about this guy, this John—"

"Miller," Mac supplied.

"Miller." As he said the name, he knew it couldn't be yet another coincidence. This man had to be connected to Devra.

"Tell him he knew Michelle."

"Riley, if you're right and John did…" Mac's voice broke. "I'll kill him, Riley. I swear on everything I have, I'll kill the son of a bitch."

"Not if I get to him first," Riley muttered.

No sound reached him from the other end of the line.

"Thanks, Mac. You've really helped."

"Riley, there's something else."

Riley's heartbeat stilled at the serious tone of Mac's voice.

"I don't blame you for what happened to Mom."

"Mac…"

"I told her where you were."

Riley didn't speak, just tried to process the meaning behind Mac's words. All these years and he'd never said a thing.

"She wouldn't have gone to the park if I hadn't told her where to find you. She died because of me."

Riley's throat squeezed shut and he could barely get the words out. "No, Mac. She died because of a doped-up kid. I think the two of us have been playing what-ifs for too many years and it hasn't done either of us any good."

Mac paused, then said, "I just wanted you to know that I don't blame you."

Riley took a deep breath as years of pent-up guilt broke free in his chest. "Thanks, Bro. You don't know how good it feels to hear you say that."

"Riley?"

"Yeah?"

"Go nail the SOB who killed my wife."

As Riley hung up the phone, he felt as if he could touch the moon. Finally they were getting somewhere. He dialed Tony's number, deciding to beat Mac to the punch. After he hung up he raced back to the chief's office. But the room was empty. "Chief Marshall!" he yelled down the hallway.

"What is it?" the chief asked as he came out of a room carrying a fresh cup of coffee.

"We've got a lead, a real good one."

"Lead in what?"

"In who killed your son."

"I know who killed my son." Chief Marshall passed him and walked into his office.

"You're wrong."

"And what about all this?" He pointed to Devra's file, to the books lying on his desk.

"I told you, she's psychic. Somehow, she's connected with the killer. She sees what he sees. That's how she knows so many details. That's why her parents think she's insane."

"Sounds insane to me."

"Hear me out for a minute," Riley insisted.

The chief leaned back in his chair. "Why not? I've been waiting fifteen years for this opportunity, and now you've brought her back to me. I can afford to give you a couple minutes."

Riley sat down and leaned across the desk. "We have a sketch of a suspect we believe could have killed Officer MacIntyre."

"MacIntyre, huh? Any relation?"

"My sister-in-law."

Surprise crossed the chief's face.

"Believe me," Riley said. "I want her killer found and convicted as much as you want Tommy's."

The chief nodded. "I'm listening."

"When Devra saw the sketch, she identified the man as the same person who killed your son."

"Mighty convenient if you ask me."

"Perhaps, but my brother also saw the sketch. He's identified him as a man he works with, a Mr. John Miller. Do you know anyone by that name?"

The chief shook his head. "Can't say that I do."

Mandy poked her head in the doorway. "Chief, sorry to interrupt, but this just came through on the fax machine. It's from a detective Tony Tortorici at the New Orleans Police Department." She walked into the room and handed him the sketch of John Miller.

"Tony's my partner. I just filled him in on the details and asked him to fax over the sketch. Have you ever seen that man before? Is there any chance he's related to Devra?"

"I've never heard of a John Miller around these parts." The chief looked thoughtful for a moment, then placed his mug and the sketch on his desk and started rifling through Devra's file. He pulled out an old sketch yellowed with age and not nearly as detailed, but they were obviously both of the same man.

The Chief stared at the two sketches, deep lines furrowing his brow. Then he looked up and said, "Fifteen years ago, Devra was so insistent that a man killed my boy that we brought a sketch artist down from Seattle to work with her." He laid the two sketches side by side and pointed to the aged paper. "This is the man she said killed my boy."

Riley looked at the sketches, a sense of foreboding racing down his spine. Even in graphite, the eyes were dark enough to make his blood run cold. They held the same evil stare as the eyes depicted in the sketch of John Miller.

"I didn't believe her. None of us did." Something broke in the chief's face, and Riley had to look away. "All these years, he's been out there killin' and I could have stopped it, I could have found justice for Tommy. Dammit!" The chief swept Devra's books and all the papers from her file off his desk. "Mandy!" he bellowed.

"Yeah, Chief," she said a little reluctantly, as she swung her head in through the opened door.

"Go into the bathroom and bring Miss Miller back in here."

Startled, Mandy stood rooted in the doorway.

"Now!"

"Could, Chief, but—er—she's not here."

Riley looked up in surprise, his gut tightening as the implications of her words set in.

"Then where the dickens is she?"

Mandy's eyes widened as her tone dissolved into a defensive whine. "She said she left something back at the hotel that she wanted you to see. She said she'd be right back. I'm sorry, Chief."

Chief Marshall looked at Riley.

He shook his head. "There was nothing."

Mandy cleared her throat. "Would you mind if I take another look at that fax from New Orleans?"

The chief handed her the fax. "Why, do you know him, Mandy?"

"No, sir, but I've seen him."

The chief stood. "When? Where?"

"Just a few minutes ago, lurking around outside on the sidewalk. Right before Miss Miller left."

Chapter Fifteen

Devra needed answers. She tried to focus on the winding road ahead of her, but tears kept filling her eyes and blurring her vision. She wasn't sure when it had happened, but she'd fallen in love with Riley. She'd even started to believe her life was going to be different. That she wouldn't have to live under a cloud of suspicion and danger, that they actually had a chance at a future together.

She'd imagined Sunday dinners with his family, going for rides on Babe, boating across the bayou, making love day and night. Fresh tears rolled down her cheeks. They might even have had children of their own. But she'd been kidding herself, and now she would pay the price.

She pulled to a stop in front of her parents' home. This time, she wouldn't leave until she learned the truth of who she was, and why they'd given her up and left her at the sanitarium. She turned off the car, then ran around the side of the house to the kitchen door. Through the window, she could see her parents sitting at the kitchen table, each lost in their own thoughts.

Her mama looked up as she pulled open the door. "Devra, you came back," she said looking pleased.

Devra didn't say a word, just walked into the kitchen and sat down across from them. "I need to know the truth. It's just us now. Spill."

Surprise and confusion crinkled her mama's brow. "What are you talking about?"

Her papa just stared, his face a blank mask.

Devra took a deep breath, then asked quickly before she lost her nerve, "Are you my parents?"

Her mother gasped. "Of course we're your parents. Your papa and I love you, Devy. I know you don't believe that, but it's true."

"You're right. I don't believe it. And the chief wants to know where I was born. Where did we live before we came here? How did I break my pinky?"

Her mama's eyes widened, her fingers fluttering up her neck to cover her mouth.

"What happened to me?" Devra asked. "Who am I?"

"We raised you," her papa said. "We tended you when you were sick, we pulled you into our bed at night when you were scared, we love you."

"But are you my parents? Did you give birth to me? I need to know, because it's the only justification I can find as to why you dumped me off in a mental institution and never came back."

An anguished moan ripped from her mama's throat and her eyes filled with tears. Devra watched her, heard her, with an odd sense of detachment. A part of her knew she should back off, knew she should give her mama a chance to pull herself together, but she couldn't.

She'd lost too much of her life to give any more, and now she'd lost Riley, too. She sighed. "Please, just tell me the truth."

Her mama stood. "We need to tell her."

"Lydia," her papa warned.

"It's time, William." Lydia walked to the closet in the hall, opened it and pulled a metal box off the top shelf way in the back.

"Don't, Lydia," her papa said, fatigue etching heavy lines into his face.

Devra stared at her papa, then focused on the box in her mother's hands. A strange trepidation kicked up her heartbeat. Her future was in that box, along with all the secrets from her past. It was the key to unlocking the nightmare that had been her life and, all this time, it'd been right there in the hall closet of her childhood home.

"I have to, William. I should have years ago. We both should have." With a thud, her mama dropped the box on the yellow Formica table, then fished in the drawer next to the refrigerator for the small key. Her hands shook as she turned open the lock and lifted the lid. Inside was a manila envelope that had discolored with time.

Suddenly, Devra was finding it difficult to breathe. Her mama sat in the chair next to her. "Your papa and I promised the Lord to love you and protect you each and every day of our lives, and we've tried to do that. That is why we chose not to tell you what I'm about to tell you now. It's only because we feel—"

William grunted.

"—I feel it would serve you better to know the truth

about your past that I'm telling you now. Because behind it all, Devra, it doesn't matter where you came from or who your parents were, because we are your family and you are loved." Tears misted her eyes.

Devra didn't respond, couldn't. A lump had formed in her throat making it difficult for her to swallow. With trembling fingers, her mama dug into the envelope and pulled out a yellowed photograph of a smiling man standing with his hands on the shoulders of a young boy. Sitting next to them was a woman bouncing a toddler on her knee. Devra took the picture from her mama's fingers.

As she looked at it, she thought she should feel something. Obviously, these people had some connection to her. But she didn't feel anything but numb. "Who are they?" she asked.

"That's my brother and his wife," her papa said.

"You have a brother?" she asked, surprised.

"He was killed a long time ago," her mama said softly. "So was his wife."

Devra stared closely at the picture, at the little baby in the frilly white dress with a head full of tight yellow curls. "Is that me?"

Her mother's eyes closed as pain filled her face. "Yes," she said softly, so softly Devra almost didn't hear her. She stared at the baby a moment longer, awed by the happy smile and chubby little legs. Then she perused the faces of her real mother and father. They looked like such nice people. They looked as if they loved her. They looked as if *they* would have fought for her.

"Why didn't you tell me you weren't my parents? Why didn't you give me the chance, give them the chance to—" She'd meant for the words to come out strong, demanding, insistent, giving them no room to back down or retreat, but at the last moment, her throat tightened and tears filled her eyes.

As they cleared, she focused on the boy in the picture. Something quivered inside her. "Who is the boy?" she asked, unable to keep the tremor out of her voice. Because she knew, deep down, she knew who the boy was.

Her mama looked at her papa, who shook his head, his eyes imploring her to keep silent.

"Tell me, Mama. Is this boy my brother?"

She nodded, some secret pain aging her face and dulling her eyes.

Devra stopped breathing. "I don't understand," she whispered. "Where is he? What happened to him?"

Taking great pains, her mama opened an old newspaper article and smoothed it across the table.

"You shouldn't have kept that, Lydia," William admonished.

Devra's stomach turned and the room tilted as the bold, black headlines leapt off the page. Thirteen-year-old Boy Bludgeons Mother and Father to Death. Baby Survives.

"You are that baby," Lydia whispered.

RILEY TURNED to the chief. "We have to find her."

"Mandy, call Mrs. Hutchinson and see if she's there. Call her parents, too, then put an APB out on Officer MacIntyre's vehicle."

Riley quickly wrote down the color, model and plate number for her. A homicidal maniac was after Devra and if Riley didn't act fast, he was going to lose her. An overwhelming sensation of helplessness overcame him. Evil wouldn't win. Not again, it couldn't.

Riley stood to grab his jacket off the coat tree by the door and stopped. "Chief, she has my gun."

"What?"

Riley's cell phone rang from his pocket.

"Riley." Tony's voice was triumphant. "John Miller's last known residence is New Orleans, before that Miami, three years before that Portland and before that Seattle. Every city where one of our murders took place."

"She's at her parents'," Mandy called.

"Tell them to keep her there," the chief ordered. "We're on our way."

Riley and Chief Marshall hurried out of the building to the chief's car.

"Sorry, Tony," Riley said into the phone. "And before that?"

"He lived in a mental institution in Idaho. They released him the year he turned twenty-three."

Riley's blood went cold. "How old was Devra when he was released?"

Riley could hear Tony doing a quick calculation. "Thirteen."

"We've got your man," he said to the chief. "Released from an Idaho mental institution the year your son died."

"Riley, he killed his parents. And get this, there was

a toddler in the house, but he didn't touch her. It was Devra, Riley. She's his sister."

"Who was that on the phone?" Devra asked.

"Mandy, down at headquarters. She wants you to stay here. The chief is on his way."

"On his way to arrest me," Devra muttered. "For murders I didn't commit. He killed Tommy." She poked the picture of her brother. "He has the same evil eyes as the man I saw in the woods that day. I told you it wasn't me, but you didn't believe me. No one believed me. You were all so quick to throw me into an institution, to tell me I was sick."

"Devra," her papa said. "We only wanted to protect you from whatever evil possessed this young man. He was a good boy, but he turned bad. He killed his parents, my brother, right after he turned thirteen. After what had happened to Tommy, we were afraid the same sickness had taken root in you. We were afraid the authorities would start poking around and everyone in town would know about the evil in your blood."

Devra looked at her papa and felt nothing but cold fury. How could he have been so misguided?

"Where is my brother now?" Out of the corner of her eye, she saw a shadow pass in front of the window. She turned, but it was gone.

"Where he's always been. At Willoughby's Mental Institution in Idaho."

Devra frowned. "Are you sure he's still there? When was the last time you checked?"

"The local police checked out your story that a man

had killed Tommy, but you barely had a description," her mama said. "You had Tommy's blood all over you, and the rock used to kill him was in your hand."

Devra blew her hair back from her face, grabbed the newspaper clipping and the pictures and slipped them back into the envelope.

"Adopting you was the best thing that ever happened to your papa and me, even after everything that happened with Tommy. We love you now as much as we did the day we brought you home to us."

"You abandoned me." She stood. "You dumped me off in that torture chamber and left me there without a second glance. You never even came for a visit."

"We did come," her mama said softly. "We came every Saturday and watched you from outside the gate. We couldn't bear to go through the week without seeing for ourselves that you were okay."

Surprised, Devra stared into her mama's red, swollen eyes. "But I don't understand. I never saw you."

"It was the doctors," her papa said. "They were afraid our presence would disturb you. They said you hadn't accepted your illness, that you were trying to hide it from them, and until you accepted you were sick, you wouldn't get better.

"You always looked so peaceful sitting under the trees, writing in your journal."

Emotion swelled in Devra's chest and rose in her throat, making it hard to speak. "I hated it inside the sanitarium— the smells, the noise. I stayed outside as often as I could."

"We just wanted to help you. We were so afraid." Her mother dropped her face into her hands and cried.

"One Saturday, we drove up there and you were gone." Her papa's eyes reddened and watered. He turned away.

Stunned, Devra sat back down. She'd never seen her papa cry. Not even the day he'd left her at the sanitarium. Tears spilled over onto her cheeks as her heart breaking overwhelmed her. She'd been wrong about them. All these years, she'd been so wrong. They did love her, they had cared.

"We didn't think we'd ever see you again," her mama said, sniffling. "But here you are, a woman with a life of your own."

"It's been a hard life, Mama. A life of always looking over my shoulder, always on the run."

"How can we help you, Devra?" her papa asked.

"I should disappear. Go where no one can find me. Especially him." She pointed to his picture once more. "What's his name?"

"Johnny. Johnny Miller," her papa said with a small shake of his head.

"Devra, you can't leave," her mama pleaded. "The chief is on his way."

"I'm not going to let them lock me up again. Chief Marshall is convinced I killed his son. But now I know different, now I know it was my brother."

"You can't spend the rest of your life running and hiding," her papa said. "You need to fight for your future."

She stared at him, afraid to trust the strength flowing through her. They believed her. "You sound like Riley."

Go back to the beginning and start from there. Riley's words whispered through her mind. "I remember this house," she said lifting the envelope. "The one in the picture. I dreamed about it earlier. I think it's all coming back. I think I'm beginning to remember what happened."

"You were too young. Barely three."

"I remember the floor, the blood." A shiver coursed through her. "I'm going back there."

"Let me go with you," her papa said.

She was tempted. But she knew what would happen if she did, and if she had to watch her papa die, she really would go insane. "I'm sorry, but this is something I have to do on my own. I'm going to find this brother of mine, and I'm going to take my life back."

"Please, Devy, let the authorities handle this," her mama pleaded.

"I wish I could. I wish I could trust them. But I don't."

"What about that young man of yours?"

"He doesn't believe in me either." The words hurt, but she knew in her heart they were true. She opened the screen door. "But I'll prove them all wrong."

Without glancing back, Devra climbed into the truck, turned on the ignition and buckled her seat belt. As she pulled down the driveway, something behind one of the tall pine trees caught her eye. As she passed, she glanced behind it, but didn't see anything. She was jumping at shadows, she thought as she settled deeper into her seat. She turned onto the main road, heading east away from Rosemont, away from the chief and away from Riley.

Riley. He was probably furious at her. She pushed

him out of her mind. The only chance she had of winning him back was to prove her innocence and for the first time in her life, she finally had something to go on, she finally had hope.

She adjusted her rearview mirror. Eyes as black as a Washington night sky stared back at her through the mirror, close enough to bore into her soul and burn her with those red glints of laughter. She stared, frozen. Her knuckles whitened as she gripped the steering wheel. Her vision shot back to the road, then back to the rearview mirror. He was gone. She imagined him, she thought, but was afraid to turn and look, afraid that she hadn't imagined him and he was actually there, waiting for her.

"What do you want?" she said, her voice quavering. Silence filled the space.

He's not there, she told herself. You imagined him. She slowed, gathering the nerve to turn and look, to see for herself that there was no one in the back seat.

"You can run, but you can't hide. Not from me."

Devra's heart slammed into her chest. She refused to look in the mirror. He was there. God help her, he was in the car. Adrenaline surged through her. She hit the brakes hard. The Expedition lurched and spun onto the shoulder. Her head slammed into the steering wheel. Pain erupted across her forehead.

She stayed like that for a long moment, afraid to move, afraid to see him. Fear quickened her blood and sent it roaring through her ears. She forced herself to lift her head from the steering wheel, to turn and look into the back seat—into the face of her nightmares.

Into the face of her brother.

He smiled—his teeth gleaming and white and perfect. "Peekaboo, Devy."

Chapter Sixteen

Stunned, Riley stared at William. "What do you mean she's gone?" Fury doused with fear surged through him. "There's a serial killer out there stalking Devra and you let her leave?"

"I'm sorry, Mr. MacIntyre, but she doesn't trust you."

"She said you don't believe in her," Lydia added.

Riley cringed. He'd had his doubts, but he hadn't said a word. How had she known?

"Any idea where she could have gone?" the chief asked.

"You gonna lock her up again?" William asked. "I won't be party to that. I just can't go through that again."

The chief sighed. "No, William. Officer MacIntyre is right. Your daughter's in danger. For Devra's sake, tell us where she is."

"She's gone to find her brother," Lydia said, her voice barely above a whisper. "She said she was going to track him down and take her life back."

"Where was she headed?" Riley asked as uneasiness churned through him. He couldn't bear to think of Devra out there trying to track down a killer alone.

"Where it all began," William said. "Jensen's Peak, about an hour east of here."

DEVRA STARED into the black depths of her brother's eyes. Eyes that had tortured her for years, every time she'd lay down to sleep. Panic sliced through her. "What do you want?" she whispered.

"I just want to play, Devy." The tinny timbre of his voice scraped across her mind. There was a wild look to his eyes, an excitement, which caused fear to constrict her chest. *What did he mean, play?*

He'd chased her through the forest the day he'd killed Tommy, he'd stood over her after she'd fallen to the ground, but had left her alive to face the wrath of a town. "Why didn't you kill me? Why everyone but me?"

"I would never hurt you, Devy. I love you."

Love me? The bottom dropped out of her stomach. "Is it true? Are you my brother?" She knew it was true, as much as she tried to deny it; she'd seen the picture, she'd read the headlines. She knew better than anyone exactly what Johnny Miller was capable of.

He smiled that perfect smile and, for a second, he almost looked normal. She could almost imagine what their lives could have been like, if only he were sane.

He touched her hair, pulling a lock of curls through his fingers. She cringed as she stared at the smooth skin of his hand. It wasn't large, callused or even dirty like she'd expect a killer's hand to be. It was just an ordinary hand, yet it had stolen so much—her parents, Tommy, her life.

He'd ripped Michelle from Mac and Riley, and all those other women, those she knew about and those she didn't. It was her brother she had the psychic connection with, her brother who'd killed anyone who'd gotten close to her, anyone who'd reminded him of her.

"I told you that you couldn't hide from me, Devy. Don't you remember when we used to play peekaboo? How you used to laugh. Laugh for me now, Devy."

She couldn't laugh. She wanted to laugh. Wanted to laugh with the maniacal glee of those poor sick souls she'd lived with in the sanitarium. But she couldn't laugh any more than she could disappear into her head to better worlds, safer worlds.

Because she was sane.

The knowledge hit her with a twisted irony. Of course she was sane. She'd always known she was sane, no matter what everyone had said to convince her differently. They'd been wrong.

He touched her shoulder, softly running his finger down her arm. She cringed, and closed her eyes.

"You've been hiding for years now," he said. "But I've always found you. And I always will. We're connected. I can see you in my dreams, see what you're doing. I can see who you're with."

Nausea rose in her throat. Had he seen her with Riley? Had he seen her alone in her house, scared out of her mind after she'd had one of her "dreams"? Is that why he continued to kill, to have that connection with her? Her stomach turned, and she knew she was going to be sick. She opened the car door and stumbled out onto the side of the road, bent over, clutching her stomach and gasping huge breaths of air.

She hurried back down the road toward her parents' house, still holding her stomach, trying to get away from him, to get away from the knowledge of who he was and what he'd done. *All because he loved her.*

She heard him get out of the car and come running up the street. He grabbed her from behind and spun her around to face him. He was happy, he was laughing, he was completely insane.

"Smile for me, Devy."

She couldn't smile any more than she could drag her gaze away from his face. She supposed it was a handsome face, so different from her own. She wondered if he took after their papa, wondered what it would have been like to have been a family, to have known her parents. To be normal. "Why did you kill our parents?" she asked, trying to make sense of the nonsensical.

He grabbed her pinky with his own and yanked hard. Pain shot through her hand. She cried out and tears filled her eyes.

"That's all that happened," he said through gritted teeth. "They said I broke your pinky. They said I couldn't play with you anymore. But I couldn't let them do that. You are mine. Mine!" He pulled her hard against his chest.

Fear, cold and sharp, snapped through her.

He lifted her chin, so she had to look at him, had to see the insanity alive in his eyes. "They had to be punished. Don't you see? I couldn't let them take you away from me. You were mine. I loved you. None of those other girls could ever be you. They tried, but they failed. They had to stop trying to play our game."

"Oh, God," she muttered.

"Come on, Devy. Smile for me, laugh."

He twisted her pinky again and the tears spilled out of her eyes and ran down her cheeks. "But what about Tommy?"

"Tommy couldn't have you. He thought he could. I know what he wanted, but he didn't get the chance. I made sure of that."

Devra swayed on her feet. The feel of him so close to her was suffocating. She pushed against his chest. "Please, let me go."

"You let that cop touch you. I saw you. He's going to have to be punished for that. You're both going to pay for that." He clutched her jaw and squeezed. "You need to know, Devra, that you're mine. No one can touch you but me. Do you understand?"

Horror and revulsion twisted inside her as the meaning behind his words hit home. "But I'm your sister."

"That makes it more special. You were meant to be mine. I've been saving myself just for you."

She was unable to comprehend how anyone could be so twisted. She looked into his dark eyes, but couldn't see anything there. Not one speck of humanity, of feeling, of compassion shone back at her. Just a black, empty abyss that made her blood run cold.

He pressed his lips softy against hers and her knees buckled. She would have fallen to a heap on the asphalt had he not lifted her up into his arms and carried her back to Riley's Expedition.

THEY DROVE for an eternity, down one winding isolated road after another. Devra sat motionless, trying not to think, wondering where Riley was and what he was thinking.

He might never find her. He might never know that it wasn't her. It had never been her. She bit back frustrated tears and tried to focus. She had to do whatever it took to get out of this situation. To get back to Riley.

"Penny for your thoughts?"

She looked over at Johnny, her brother, her own personal devil. "Where are you taking me?"

"Home."

"My home's in New Orleans."

Something cold and angry moved in his eyes. "Your home's with me. No one will ever take you away from me again. We're going to live there with Mom and Dad, just like we used to."

"Mom and Dad?" she squeaked.

He smiled. "They're waiting for us. It's time to go home now. All the fun and games are over."

Devra started to rock. *What did he mean, They're waiting for us?* Suddenly, she was certain she didn't want to know.

They pulled off onto a gravel road that led deep into the forest. As the branches parted, a rundown small wooden structure came into view. She'd seen that house before—in the picture her mama had shown her and in her dreams. An image teased her, flitting in and out of her memories. She knew what the inside of that house would look like, knew that the floors would gleam....

"I can't go in there," she said in a voice barely above a whisper.

"This is our home. This is where we'll live from now on. No one will ever bother us here. I'll take care of you, just like I used to."

"You can't keep me here. My parents know where I am. Riley will find me."

He looked at her and smiled, suddenly looking normal again. Suddenly looking as if he were in complete control and knew exactly what he was doing. "No one will find you. I'm going to take care of everything, just like always."

Confusion twisted around her and pulled tight.

"Devra Miller disappeared a long time ago, and Devra Morgan doesn't exist."

"But, Riley—"

He laughed. "That foolish cop only thinks about his mommy. He doesn't know she walks beside him all the time, looking sad, looking heartbroken. Don't you see it will set them both free? Then they can be together, they can be happy. Like us. Like families should."

He got out of the truck and walked around to open her door. She didn't move. Couldn't. Something cold had taken control of her limbs. Was it possible? Were the dead constantly around us? Could he really see them?

He grabbed her arm and pulled. She almost fell out of the truck, found her footing and righted herself. "Please," she whispered. "Please don't make me go in there."

Blood. If she closed her eyes, she could see it inching across the floor, filling the seams, darkening the wood.

He pushed her toward the door, opened it and forced her in. The floor wasn't golden or gleaming, it was old and weathered and beyond repair. A rat scurried across the room, making her skin crawl.

"We can't live here!" she cried. A dark corner of her mind beckoned. A deep abyss where there was no light, no thought, no visions. It was someplace she could go, her mind whispered, someplace she could hide.

He continued toward the kitchen. She stood rooted in the doorway, refusing to move. Then she saw the table set up in the corner, with the lace tablecloth and wooden bowl. So much like the one Tommy was carrying that day. Something red stained the inside of the bowl. Raspberries? Blood?

Next to the bowl sat a baby dress and hairbrush, an old stuffed bear and a music box, the kind with a crank where the lid opens and a clown pops out. As she stared at the box, a chill worked its way inside her and she began to tremble. "Please," she whispered.

"Mama, Papa, we're home!" he yelled.

Horrified, she stared at her brother. "They're not here," she insisted.

He turned to her. "Of course they're here. They've been waiting for you." He grabbed her arm and pulled.

Please don't let them be here, she begged. The room shifted and as she moved closer to the kitchen doorway, she could almost see her mother lying on the floor, her long golden curls resting in a puddle of blood.

Her brother turned to her, his eyes glazing over—the

blank dead stare of a corpse. "They're right there in front of you. In the kitchen, can't you see them?"

The warped music box began to play.

"No," she whispered, shaking her head.

"We're a family again, now that I've brought you back home."

A shudder passed through her. *He was never going to let her go.*

"Let's go into the nursery and play."

As he reached for her, images from the past circled round her. Suddenly she couldn't tell which images were her memories and which were fragments from his shattered mind. "Stay away from me."

He tugged her harder. "Come on, Devy! Let's play."

"No!" she screamed, placing her hands over her ears to block out the music box, to block out the screams of a toddler crying for her mommy.

The room spun.

She turned and ran out the door, away from the house, away from the nightmare.

Away from him.

"You can run, but you can't hide, Devy! I can always find you!"

She ran. Like so many times before. But she knew it was no use. She knew he would find her, he always did. Despair choked her. Her parents knew where she was. He was there, he knew that. Would he kill them, too? *Riley.* Pain and fear squeezed her heart, and she doubled over as the breath choked in her throat. He was going to kill them all.

Sobs racked her soul. Suddenly, she heard the whisper of water moving on the breeze, pushing through the trees, circling around her and she knew what she had to do, where she had to go.

It was her only chance.

Chapter Seventeen

"There's my truck," Riley said as they rounded the corner and saw his Expedition pulled up in front of an old, abandoned house.

"We'd better park back here and walk in," the chief said.

Riley agreed. The front door was wide open and the house was too quiet, making him edgy. The chief handed him a gun and they moved in and made a quick sweep of the house. No one was inside.

"Damn!" Riley muttered, stopping as he spotted a gun on the old, splintered mantel above the fireplace.

"Yours?" the chief asked.

Sickness twisted inside Riley's stomach as he said, "Michelle's."

"Good, then it's possible Devra still has yours. Let's split up and head into the woods." The chief turned, but stopped in front of a small table in the corner. His hand trembled as it hovered over a wide, decorative bowl. "I haven't seen this bowl since…" The chief didn't finish the thought.

Next to the bowl were several little girl things: a dress, a hairbrush, a broken music box. Instinctively, Riley knew they were Devra's. An angry sense of frustration overwhelmed him. She'd been this man's obsession for years. He had to find her.

He remembered something she'd said about feeling cold, and her dream about drowning. "Is there a river around here?"

"Yeah, back behind the house," the chief said still staring at the bowl.

"Let's start there."

DEVRA KNEW John was behind her. She could hear him laughing, could hear him enjoying himself. One last fatal chase through the woods. Despair threatened to overwhelm her. She was running again. She'd always be running.

"Caught you, Devy!" John said as he grabbed her arm and spun her around. "I always will." He pulled her against him. Suddenly, his smile disappeared and his face screwed up into a mask of hate and anger. He yanked at her skirt, almost ripping the fabric. "What is this?" he asked, holding up Riley's gun.

She closed her eyes as her last hope was ripped from her pocket. He pushed the muzzle up under her chin. "Little girls shouldn't play with guns."

She stared him in the eye, but didn't say a word. For a moment, he watched her, then he let her go. He chucked the gun into the woods. As he did she turned and, not knowing where she'd go or what she'd do, ran toward the river. It wasn't far now, she could hear it whispering through the trees.

"Devy!" he yelled.

Her stomach flip-flopped at the maniacal intensity of his roar. She could see the water now—sparkling, inviting. This river was so much wider than the one by her parents' home, the current much stronger. Not far downstream, a large bridge crossed to the other side. She ran toward the bridge and up the embankment, her legs burning, her chest heaving.

"Stay away from there, Devy!" He was gaining on her. "You know you're not allowed up there." An edge of panic entered his voice.

She reached the top and ran out onto the bridge. She thought she heard Riley calling her name. But that couldn't be, could it? Hope filled her, but she pushed it away. She had to keep her head. No one was there to save her, no one ever had been.

Within seconds, John was on the bridge, moving closer. "You know better than to come out on the bridge. Mama and Papa have told you many times." Panic twisted into anger and fury filled his face. "You're going to have to be punished, Devy."

The dead calm in his tone as he said the words turned her blood cold. He stepped toward her and she knew she was going to die. This time, he would kill her. She'd seen that deadly look in his eyes too many times before—in her dreams. Fear and helplessness choked her. She held tight to the rail to keep from plummeting into the fast-moving river.

"Please, John, if you ever loved me, let me go."

He stopped and stared at her, his head cocked to the side as if he didn't quite understand. "Love you, Devy? I'm the only one who has ever truly loved you. I've brought you back home. I'm giving you back your family."

She shook her head as tears burned the backs of her eyes. There would be no escaping him, nothing she could do.

"Devra!"

Devra gasped, her eyes searching the trees. "Riley, over here!"

John's face distorted into a mask of hate. "You will not have him," he said through clenched teeth. "Do you understand, you will only be with me?"

Riley ran out of the forest and onto the river's path. The sight of him filled Devra's heart with joy. He was coming for her. Everything would be all right now. He'd come for her. Happy tears filled her eyes.

"It's over, John," she said softly.

He stepped toward her, something cold and deadly moving in his eyes. Suddenly he lunged, grabbing her, pulling her up against him. "It will never be over," he gritted, then lifted her off her feet and threw her over the side of the bridge.

Devra screamed with panic, then gulped a deep breath. Ice-cold water shocked her system as she plunged below the surface. She closed her eyes and let the numbing coldness wash over her as she sunk farther toward the bottom. Don't panic, she told herself. Riley's here. Riley will save her.

As the current grabbed hold and tried to sweep her

downstream, her eyes flew open. She couldn't let that happen. She had to stay close to Riley. As she passed by one of the bridge's large metal pilings, she hooked her legs around it and held on tight against the current.

A splash sounded above her, sending shock waves through the water. She peered through the darkness. Riley? Her heart squeezed painfully at the sight of her brother. She held tight to the piling and tried to fade into the shadows, hoping the current would carry him past her downstream. His dark gaze locked on hers as he swept by her. He reached for her, his long, bony hand stretching.

She cringed, pulling back as far as she could. Luckily, he sped past her. Lack of oxygen burned her chest. Her eyes widened as she saw him in the gloom kicking his strong legs, pushing toward her. *Lord, help me.* She tried to climb the piling, but the current was too strong and she was too tired. *Riley, where are you!*

Her brother was so close now. She could see the fatigue filling his face as he swam against the current to reach her. Her strength waned. It took everything she had to cling to the piling, to concentrate on staying calm. Riley would be there soon, he would save her. She couldn't let go. If she did, she'd be swept downstream and lost forever.

Her eyes widened as John closed the distance separating them. Before she could think of what she could do to fight him, he wrapped his arms around her in a fierce hold. She didn't have the strength to struggle. Instead, she focused on keeping her legs wrapped around the piling, refusing to let him pull her free.

Cold determination entered his eyes. She wasn't sure

where she got the strength to hold on to the piling, and on to him. Suddenly, it was so easy. He struggled against her, but she held tight thinking of all the lost years, all because of her brother who loved her too much. She could have laughed at the irony. She'd always thought she was alone and unloved, but he had been there, watching, waiting, playing his sick games the whole time.

Her limbs began to grow weak and her mind started to drift as the burn increased, then dissipated, in her chest. Suddenly, she realized she wasn't cold anymore as languid warmth moved through her. She saw something coming toward her—a bright, golden light moving steadily through the dark haze.

Mama?

Joy filled every part of her and she realized she'd never felt this happy before, this complete. She looked into John's eyes to see if he saw her, too. But his dark gaze had lost its sheen and seemed to be focused on nothing at all.

You were right, John. Mama is here! She is waiting for me. She opened her arms to embrace her mother and barely noticed as John drifted away.

Mama, I'm home.

"No!" RILEY'S HEART screamed as he watched the man throw Devra over the side of the bridge. He wouldn't let her leave him. He couldn't. He loved her, dammit.

He hurried to the shore, all the while watching for her to surface, but she didn't. A second later, the man followed her. Fear clutched Riley's heart, but he wouldn't succumb to it. He wouldn't let evil win, not this time. He kicked off his shoes and scanned the river for any sign of them. Where were they? Unable to wait a second longer, he dove into the water.

The first thing to hit him was the numbing cold that froze his limbs and stung his skin, the second was the murky darkness. He couldn't see two feet in front of him. Hopeless despair seized him. He surfaced.

"Anything?" the chief yelled.

"I can't see a thing!" Riley called, then dove back under and let the current take him down toward the bridge, to the last place he saw her. His heart plummeted as he searched the murky water. The current was so strong she could be a mile downstream by now. Despair clutched him and he tried to fight it. He wouldn't let another person he cared about die, especially not her—not his Devra. He loved her and he refused to live without her.

Coming up for a deep breath, he dove under again and this time, he saw something. Suddenly, the silt in the water cleared and there she was in front of him, clinging to her brother, each holding on to one another in an awkward embrace. Devra's hair billowed around them in the icy water. He wanted to yell, to scream, to breathe. His lungs ached with the effort to swim toward them.

As he approached, Devra raised her arms and let go of her brother. He drifted away, his eyes opened wide in a stupefied, blank stare. Riley reached toward her. She was looking past him and smiling. He grabbed hold of her by the waist and hauled her toward the surface.

As they broke free, he gasped a huge breath of air, but Devra didn't. She was unconscious. As fast as he was able, he swam downstream toward shore.

"She's not breathing!" he yelled to the chief as he carried her onto shore. He bent over her, grasped both arms around her waist and lifted her up, over and over, squeezing the water from her lungs. Once the water was clear, he laid her on the ground and started CPR. "Come on, Devra. Breathe," he demanded in between breaths.

"The paramedics will be here in a few minutes," the chief said and looked anxiously behind him toward the road.

Devra coughed and water came pouring out of her mouth.

Riley helped her clear the water then continued CPR until she started to cough again. "Breathe for me, baby," Riley pleaded. "Come on and breathe."

Tears streamed from her eyes as she turned to look at him. Relief overwhelmed him at the sight of her vivid blue gaze fixated on him.

"The paramedics are here," the chief said as the truck pulled near.

"You're going to be okay," Riley said.

"My mom?" She looked around, confusion filling her eyes and wrinkling her brow. "John?"

"Gone. He can't hurt you anymore. He can't hurt anyone." A shadow fell over her eyes, stealing their brightness and replacing it with a dull gleam. Riley didn't like the look of her cold, distant stare. It was almost as if the Devra he knew, the Devra inside, just disappeared. "Devra?"

"Excuse me, sir," one of the paramedics said and bent over her. "We need to check her."

Reluctantly, Riley moved out of the way as the team checked her vitals, put an oxygen mask over her face, then loaded her into the ambulance.

"Ride with them to the hospital," the chief said and nudged Riley toward their van.

"What about you?"

"I'm not leaving until I find the man who killed my boy."

"He was drifting downstream," Riley said. Then he climbed into the back of the ambulance and took Devra's hand. "It's going to be all right now. The nightmare is over," he whispered, trying to assure her that everything was okay. But he didn't like the dark cast to her gaze nor the way he couldn't get her to focus on him. It made him edgy, it gave him the feeling that everything wasn't okay, and if he weren't careful, it would never be okay again.

DARKNESS SWIRLED around her. She waited patiently for the light, for her mama to come back to her. She was cold and alone, but she wasn't scared. Somehow, it was comforting here. There was no fear, no running; she'd finally found someplace to hide where no one could find her. No one could hurt her.

She thought she felt someone touching her face, her hair. *Mama? Are you here? I'm so tired, Mama.* The shadows drifted away and she fell back to sleep.

"Devra, can you hear me?"

She stirred. *Who was that?* A voice reached for her.

She retreated back farther from the voice. She wasn't ready. *Not yet, please.*

"What's wrong with her?" the voice asked. "Why won't she wake up?"

She heard something far from her; it sounded like the rattling of papers. Then a bright light shone in her eyes. Panic tripped her heart. Stay away from me, she begged. But no one seemed to hear her. She retreated and all was black again. All was safe.

RILEY WATCHED Devra grow paler and more withdrawn with each passing hour. She was leaving him. He could feel it. Despair racked his body. This was his fault. She'd needed him, depended on him, and he'd let her down. He'd failed.

"I'm so sorry," he said softly. He squeezed her hand and pushed her wild hair back from her head. "Don't leave me, Devra. Please, come back to me."

No sound, no movement. She just lay there motionless, like a lost princess from a fairy tale. Only he wasn't her Prince Charming. Far from it. But he did love her with all his heart.

"I love you. You can't leave me. I don't want to go through this life without you. I don't want to be alone. Not anymore."

She didn't respond. He rose and stared out the window. A storm had moved in and rain was falling in sheets onto the hospital parking lot. He turned back to her. "Your mom and dad are here. They've been here all night, taking turns talking to you, holding your hand. They love you, baby, and so do I. We all love you."

He stared at the monitor that measured her heartbeat. Steady rhythms, no change, no stress, no sign that would tell him she was fighting to find her way back to him.

"I'm sorry I doubted you," he said, hoping that somehow, somewhere, she could hear him. "It was only for an instant, but it was enough to send you chasing off after that monster alone. I'll never forgive myself for that, for letting you down."

He sat back down and took her hand into both of his. "I should have trusted my instincts. I've made so many mistakes and I haven't allowed myself to learn from them and let them go. I haven't allowed myself to leave the past in the past. If I had, maybe I would have been able to trust you, your instincts, your decisions."

He dropped his forehead onto her hand. "I didn't believe in you. I gave you no choice but to fight your battle alone. That wasn't right. You shouldn't have had to face him alone."

Her hand moved.

He looked up. Was it possible? She looked the same as before; had he imagined it? "Devra? Can you hear me? Come on, sweetie. Come back to me." He stared at her hand, willing it to move again.

"No," she said, her voice a hoarse whisper that could barely be heard.

He looked up, his heart soaring as she opened her eyes.

"Not your fault," she said as tears and pain filled her eyes.

"Shh. Save your strength." Emotion overwhelmed him as he stared at her. He knew he should call a doctor, but he didn't want to let her out of his sight. "Are you okay? How are you feeling?"

"My fault. I held on. I… I didn't want to go with him." She closed her eyes and turned away.

He didn't understand. "No," he said suddenly afraid she would leave him again. "I'm going to get a doctor." He stood.

She turned back to him. "No, don't leave me. Not yet."

Hesitantly, he turned from the door then sat back down. "Are you sure you're okay?"

She stared at him for a long minute, her liquid blue eyes melting with pain. "No, I'm not okay. I don't think I'll ever be okay. I'm damaged, much more than I ever thought."

Fear clutched his heart. "What are you saying?" You're fine. There was no damage."

She closed her eyes and took a deep breath. "That's not what I mean."

Understanding dawned. "It wasn't your fault. He was a monster, yes, but it had nothing to do with you."

"It had everything to do with me. Everything he did was for me. Because of me."

"I'm sorry you had to fight him alone."

She let out a harsh sound that almost sounded like a laugh. "I didn't fight him. I ran."

"You didn't have a choice."

"Didn't I?" She sighed. "We all have choices, Riley. All these years…" Something broke in her throat. "I was loved," she whispered.

"You still are," he said softly.

She looked at him, a flicker of fear shining in her gaze.

"I love you, Devra."

"You can't," she whispered.

"I do."

"It's not safe to love me. Bad things happen to people who love me."

"Not anymore." He stood up, bent over the bed and took her face in his hands, then pressed his lips to hers. It was a frenzied kiss, desperate and unrelenting. He wouldn't let her go. Not now, not ever. "All these years, I've been afraid to love, afraid to live. Afraid if I did, life would steal it away and I wouldn't be able to live with that. But I wasn't living, any more than you were."

He sat back down and took her hand, then leaned close so she could see the sincerity in his eyes, so she could see how much this meant to him. How much she meant to him. "We were both running and hiding, not only from monsters but from love. Don't run anymore, Devra. Let me love you the way you deserve to be loved."

A tear slipped from the corner of her eye. She shook her head. "I don't know how."

"We'll figure it out together. Let go of the shame and the guilt. I have, and you can, too. But most of all, let go of the fear."

Uncertainty filled her eyes.

"Do you love me?" he asked. Anxiety pricked him as he waited for her answer. She had his heart in her hands, and he prayed she would keep it.

She nodded, slowly at first, then a small smile trembled at the corners of her lips.

He took a deep breath and a giant leap of faith. "Will

you marry me, Devra Morgan Miller? Will you stay by my side always and never let me give up fighting for you, for us, for our family?"

Tears pooled in her eyes and ran down her cheeks. "On one condition."

He had her, he could tell by the color filling her cheeks. He flashed his famous MacIntyre grin, known to melt hearts all over the South. "And what would that be, sugar?"

"That we don't fight any more monsters alone. Real, imagined or otherwise."

He leaned over the bed and pulled her into his arms, then held tight to the rest of his life. "You're on, baby."

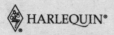

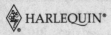

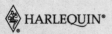

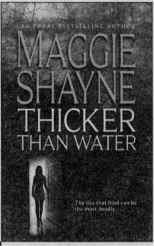